# Thief, Acolyte, Consort
By James Robert Paige

Copyright ©2020 James Paige

Copyright © 2020 James Robert Paige

All rights reserved. No part of this book may be reproduced in any form or by any electronic or mechanical means, including information storage and retrieval systems, without permission in writing from the publisher, except by reviewers, who may quote brief passages in a review.

ISBN: 978-1-7771256-0-8

Cover Art
THE KING IS DEAD, LONG LIVE THE KING
by:
Raymond Tan
http://r-tan.deviantart.com/

Published by James Robert Paige

https://linktr.ee/jamespaige

https://james.hamsterrepublic.com/writing/

Thief

◊

Acolyte

◊

Consort

# City

Catt Zago climbed up on the roof of a shack next to the Caravan Depot and surveyed her new surroundings.

It was a beautiful morning in the cursed city of Great Bakak. The rising sun cast striking shadows on the mountains behind the city, and the sky above the vast desert was clear and crisp.

She could see big marble temples and palaces on the foothills. To the west she could see geometric patches of green, the vibrant contrast to the reds and browns of the desert were a welcome sight, although they looked small in relation to the sprawling city.

In the east she could see a jumble of distant buildings with odd archways and too many towers. This was probably the wizard university that she had heard other travellers talking about.

The rest of the space between the mountains and the desert was filled with smaller, less impressive buildings, most two or three stories tall, sun-weathered gray slums with narrow unseen streets lacing between them. Somewhere nearby over the next sand dune were numerous thin columns of smoke, and the smell of roast spiced meat was on the air.

The city was big and alive, and it looked so much better than she had hoped to find at the end of such a long and desolate road. She didn't give the desert a second look before climbing back down off the roof and slipping away from the caravan without paying the safe-arrival fee.

# Signposts

A cobble-paved road led towards the heart of the city from the Caravan Depot. It was lined with signs welcoming visitors.

**"Welcome To Great Bakak"**
**"Sacred Jewel of Flal-Shom"**
**"Keep Our Capital Clean"**
**"Shop Outer Bakak Fine Meats & Sausages"**

Catt stopped in front of a large sign labelled "Know Our Laws". It was adorned by a blue crest featuring an axe above a crown. Catt grinned as she read it. The sign summarized the local rules so tourists could stay out of trouble. Most of it was very standard fare.

**"No murdering"**
**"No dueling without a permit"**
**"Don't insult the King"**
**"Stolen goods are taxable income"**
**"Magic without consent is assault!"**

A few more unique rules caught her eye near the bottom of the sign.

**"Wasting water is a crime! We have been in a drought over 1000 years"**
**"Fire is forbidden in all parts of the city where fire is possible. Constrain all fire to the Smokefields"**

Catt shook her head in amusement, and walked on.

As she walked, she looked at the people on the street. There were all kinds. She saw tall and short, men and women and everything besides. There were so many kinds of beautiful on display. There were people with fangs, people with scales, dark skin, light skin, and hair of every color in the rainbow. After spotting a few children with horns playing on the steps of a building, Catt removed the silk scarf from her head that she had wrapped every morning to conceal her own horns. In a world full of magic and gods and monsters and genetics there were always a few people who had them, and she was pleased to learn this wasn't the sort of place where you got into trouble for having them.

Catt knew it might just be her good mood tinting her perceptions, but it seemed like people she passed on the street were happy. She saw lots of smiles. An ox-cart driver was singing a cheerful song in a language she didn't recognize. A pack of children was playing some sort of stick-and-ball game in the middle of the street, and nobody seemed to mind. Someone was whistling as they hung laundry out a second floor window.

Catt turned a corner, and her heart skipped as she recognized a figure who was obviously some kind of a cop. He was wearing a black coat and hood, and his face was obscured behind a wooden mask. On his chest was the same blue axe-over-crown crest that she had seen on the "Know Our Laws" sign. On his belt was a short-handled battle-axe, gleaming sharp.

Catt was suddenly burningly aware of the sword hanging at her own belt, and of the small handful of gold coins concealed in her shirt, the last remnants of the treasure she had stolen many months ago in another city in another country in another part of the world.

The cop just nodded at her, a polite little bow that conveyed through body language the smile that might be hidden under the wooden mask.

Catt replied to the gesture with a nod of her own and an awkward little wave, and she hurried on her way, relieved.

# Blessings

High Priest Lemmy struck the lead barbarian in the face with the Flail of Destiny. He then struck each of the other two barbarians in the faces one after the other.

Although Lemmy had swung the Flail of Destiny with the full strength of his diminutive arms, none of the barbarians looked noticeably injured.

Tears trickled from the eyes of the barbarian leader, vanishing into his beard. "Thank you, your holiness!" he exclaimed, thickly accented voice cracking. "It has been so long since we have had a proper blessing!"

Lemmy bowed his head and said, "May Kruller's rage fill your hearts forever!"

Lemmy climbed down from atop the altar. Without its added height, he was no longer at eye level with his clients. His scaly snout barely came up past the barbarians' knees.

"You smote us so gently!" said one, with admiration quavering in his voice. "Just like my grandmother used to!"

The barbarians each dropped a few coins in the offering box as they left the temple.

Lemmy crossed them out of his appointment book, and stowed the Flail of Destiny away in his big cabinet of ceremonial weapons. Like the flail, most of them he had crafted himself from military surplus weapons, gilt paint, glue, and costume jewelry.

"And that's the last one for today. Praise you all!" Lemmy said, gesturing vaguely all around him. He scuttled over to the temple doors, and flipped over the "Closed" sign in the clear patch at the bottom of the stained glass window.

Before he could find his keys to lock the doors, a woman pulled them back open again and peeked her head through.

"Hey! Is this the Polypantheonic Temple?"

"Affirmative!" chirped Lemmy, with pride. "All blessings to you, and how may I help you?"

"I found one of your brochures," she said, stepping inside the temple. She was tall, and dressed like some kind of mercenary, with a sword at her side, and some glimpses of light leather armor peeking out of the edges of her blouse. She had a messy shock of short red hair on her head, with two little horns protruding from it. Her face was friendly, and her eyes seemed to be smiling, independently of her mouth.

She was holding a sheet of paper. Lemmy immediately recognized it as one of the advertisements he had printed up at the Movable Type.

"Are you mayhaps inquiring after a specific god or goddess?" he asked.

"Not really," she said, looking around as if admiring the decor. "I'm new in town, and I thought you could recommend one to me."

"Grand!" exclaimed Lemmy, with genuine pleasure. "You have come to the right place! I was just about to close the temple for the day, but for you, I have time. Come, sit!" He gestured to one of the benches. "My name is Lemmy, High Priest and founder of the Polypantheonic Temple. How should I address you, miss?"

The woman sat on the edge of the pew, and shook the clawed hand that Lemmy offered. Now that she was sitting, Lemmy didn't need to stretch upward for this greeting.

"You can call me Catt," she said.

"Enchanted, Catt. Now let's figure out what sort of deity is a good match for your personality. First, what is the most important thing in your life?"

"Starting with the easy questions, huh?" Catt asked, bemused.

"Not to worry," Lemmy chuckled. "Let me ask differently... What do you expect a god to give to *you*?"

"Hmm..." Catt stared at the rafters as she thought. Finally she said, "Good luck, I guess? I'd like somebody putting their fingers on the scale in my favor once in a while."

"Good. That's good," said Lemmy. "Now, have you ever been devoted to any gods in the past?"

"Not really," Catt replied with a shrug. "Nobody consistently."

"That's fine," said Lemmy. "Are you attached to any geo-spatial domains?"

"Geo spatial?" Catt asked, wrinkling her nose.

"Are there any regions or cities that you have a strong emotional connection with?" Lemmy clarified. "Such as where you were born or raised?"

Catt shook her head. "Nothing like that. I moved around a lot when I was young." She frowned, and added, "It wasn't great."

"Not to worry," soothed Lemmy. "Let us attempt an exercise. Take a deep breath, and imagine a peaceful and serene place."

"Okay," Catt agreed. She leaned back and partially closed her eyes. Lemmy could see that she was still peering through her lashes. He waited silently, watching her breathe, until he intuited that she looked sufficiently serene.

"Are you there?" Lemmy asked softly.

Catt nodded slightly.

"This place, are you alone in it? Or are other people around?" Lemmy asked.

"Just me..." Catt said. "But it doesn't feel lonely."

"Please describe the things you see nearby," instructed Lemmy.

"Trees..." Catt started. She hesitated and then continued, "...like shady trees. There are dry leaves on the ground. The sun is shining between the leaves."

"Is there any water around?" asked Lemmy.

"No... dew on the leaves I guess. No river or lake or anything."

"Good. Now..." Lemmy dropped the gentleness from his voice. His words became a bit harder. "A wall appears. It separates you from the trees."

Catt frowned.

"What is the wall made of?" He asked quickly.

"Fire," Catt replied.

Lemmy raised a scaly eyebrow. He was expecting "Stone," or "Bricks."

"What is your action?" Lemmy asked.

Catt's frown deepened. Her breathing was now short. Anything but relaxed. "I don't ... know..." she replied haltingly.

Lemmy waited for a moment to see if she would think of anything. After no further response was forthcoming, he said, "Very good! Excellent! Please open your eyes."

Catt opened her eyes and readjusted her posture on the bench. She seemed to take only a moment to shake off the mood of the exercise.

"Last question now," said Lemmy, cheerfully. "Have you, or anyone you love ever been cursed directly by a god."

"Um... not that I know of," Catt said, adding with a chuckle, "I think I probably pissed off a Srappan sun-god pretty badly once... I'd rather not say why."

"Curses leveled by clergy or devouts don't count in this case, I'm only concerned with curses that came directly from a divine source."

"Then no," said Catt. "I think I would have noticed that." Her eyes had regained their smiling look.

Lemmy thought about Catt's answers. Recommending a god to someone was an art, not a precise science. Lemmy had the feeling that Catt would be highly compatible with just about any benevolent trickster or mother-of-the-hunt he might recommend to her, but he didn't want to give her vague and indecisive advice.

"Give me a moment of consideration," Lemmy said as he scurried over to his bookshelf and drew back the bright tapestry curtain that concealed it.

"Alright," Catt responded.

Lemmy fetched his book of summaries and his cross-reference. Both were well-worn notebooks that he had compiled himself. They were on the bottom shelf with all the most important volumes that he needed to be able to consult quickly without bothering with the ladder.

He had a few good ideas already, but wanted to be sure.

After a few minutes of looking things up in the aspect index, Lemmy glanced up and saw that Catt had moved from the bench. She was now sitting cross-legged on the floor close to the stained glass window. She seemed to be watching the distorted silhouettes of people walking past on the street.

"Hey, is something happening today?" Catt asked suddenly. "I noticed all afternoon there have been people dressed up nice and all walking in the same direction."

"Ah! Yes, you are new to our fine city!" said Lemmy. "Today is the Regicide Feast. It is the most important festival on our calendar."

"Am I making you late for it?" Catt asked.

"Not at all," Lemmy reassured. "I still have plenty of time."

Lemmy flipped back and forth between two pages comparing two entries, when another name in the cross reference caught his eye. "Ah! Perhaps!" he muttered to himself, following the reference and skimming the description.

Lemmy looked at Catt again. She was still people-watching through the stained glass.

"Miss Catt! I believe you have a spider on your arm," Lemmy lied.

Catt lifted her arm and inspected her shoulder and elbow. She didn't slap at herself or show any sign of panic, just curiosity. She checked the other arm, "Where? I don't see it."

"My mistake," said Lemmy. "Must have been a mere trick of the light."

That clenched it. Lemmy put away his summaries and cross references. He wheeled over his ladder and fetched a small book from the top shelf.

Lemmy came to where Catt was sitting. "Consider praying to Hret-ret-akl," he suggested. "She is a forest spirit goddess. Her geo-spatial domain is on the far side of the mountains." He pointed northward. "She manifests as a faceless, formless, many-limbed cloud. Her influence includes sprouting seeds, crawling bugs, rotting food, and unlucky circumstances."

"She sounds awful!" Catt said with a grimace, "Besides, I want *good* luck, not *bad* luck."

"Hear me out," Lemmy entreated. "A god of good luck is fine for gamblers, but good luck is already its own reward. And patron deities of good fortune tend to want a portion of those benefits returned back to them in one way or another. Hret-ret-akl is different. She offers her worshipers no promises to prevent bad luck– rather, when unlucky circumstances befall you, she can help those circumstances affect you in meaningful ways you won't expect."

Catt just frowned, but in a way that looked more thoughtful than displeased.

Lemmy continued. "And don't let yourself be put off by her aspects of decay. The insects, the rotting, these are very typical of a forest spirit, and they show her connection to cycles of life and death. That means she cares about mortals, and is more likely to take notice of your prayers."

Catt's lips were still frowning just a little, but her eyes were radiating smile again.

"Okay, maybe," Catt said.

"Take this book," Lemmy instructed, pressing it into Catt's hand. "You can borrow it. It has a chapter about her."

Catt took the book from Lemmy's outstretched claw.

# Festival

Catt tucked the book into her pack. She had come here simply because the flier advertising the Polypantheonic Temple seemed like a fun and interesting scam, and she had been curious what sort of grifter was behind it. Now that she had met him, Catt liked the sincere little lizard-man who called himself a High Priest. She wasn't so sure anymore that this "Temple" was a grift.

"Thank you," she said. "I suppose you have to get ready for that festival now?"

"Yes," agreed Lemmy. "I must find my good hat." He began rummaging around in the bottom of a large wooden wardrobe in the corner of the temple. Its exterior was hand painted with a jumble of various holy symbols.

"Can just anybody go to this festival?" Catt asked.

"Yes! All are welcomed!" said Lemmy from inside the wardrobe. "You should attend! It is an important local tradition that marks the new year on our calendar. If you please, we can walk there together, and I shall show you where to get the best food."

"I'm not sure I can afford the best food," Catt countered.

"The food is all free," Lemmy clarified. "The King provides it."

"What, the King feeds the whole city?"

Lemmy emerged from the wardrobe bearing a huge feathered mitre. The headpiece was nearly as tall as he was.

"I would estimate that approximately one third of the city attends the festival on any given year," Lemmy answered, wrestling a tiny white-and-silver sequined robe onto his diminutive shoulders. "It's certainly a serious culinary undertaking, the King pays every kitchen in the Smokefields to cater it, and they compete for the honor of outdoing one another."

Catt grinned. "Okay, I can't miss this."

Then, after considering Lemmy's garish robe and towering hat she asked, "Am I going to be underdressed at this event?"

Lemmy chuckled, "As a High Priest, I must look the part, besides… with this fine hat, perhaps tall-folk will be less likely to trip over my personage in the crowd."

Catt waited outside while Lemmy locked the front door of the temple. From the outside, the Polypantheonic Temple looked like a temple-themed storefront. To either side were ordinary shops, and the second floor seemed to be the windows of apartments.

Catt and Lemmy walked towards the festival. People frequently greeted Lemmy, and he seemed to know them all by name.

"Good day, Your Holiness!"

"Good day, Mr Marglov! How is your granddaughter?"

"Much better! Thank you for asking."

Another man stooped to shake Lemmy's hand. "Nirgosh bless you, Reverend!"

"Nirgosh bless you as well my son."

Different people seemed to use a wide variety of different honorifics to address Lemmy.

"Shaman Lemmy! Good to see you!"

"Good to see you as well, Mrs Basts. We missed you at Wailing And Chanting practice."

"I was under the weather that night, Shaman, I'll be there next time."

After listening to people address Lemmy variously as Cleric, Vicar, Divine, Heirophant, and Pontiff, Catt asked, "What actually is your proper title?"

Lemmy chuckled, "It depends on which deities one reveres, and which sort of religious tradition I provide them services in... but mostly I just let people call me what they please."

"Do you mind if I call you Lemmy?"

"That would be just fine," Lemmy answered with a toothy smile. "Please do."

They passed into a part of the city where the style of buildings was different. These were bigger, more imposing, less inviting buildings. There were marble facades, carved decorative embellishments, grand columns and archways. The crowds also grew more dense here. Everyone was moving in the same direction.

Finally they reached a huge open square. On the opposite end of the square was a glittering palace, and the sides of the square were lined with grandiose temples, banks, and guildhalls.

The square was teeming with people of every description. The combined noise of voices was a full roar that mixed together with the music being played by a small orchestra set up on the steps of one of the temples. A few trees rose up above the crowd, evenly spaced, hinting at the shape of the park in the middle of the square.

Lemmy led the way, skirting the thickest part of the crowd, and staying close to one row of trees. Here many families had brought blankets and were setting up picnics. Children played and laughed, and white-clad porters pushed wheeled carts laden with small baskets of food that were distributed to the crowd.

Catt could smell delicious scents of roasted and spiced dishes. She was conscious of being hungry.

"Don't be tempted aside," advised Lemmy. "Certainly that food is good, but the best will be up ahead."

Past the last of the trees were steps leading up to a higher terraced area directly in front of the palace. This area was full of long tables, where people were sitting and feasting.

Lemmy continued, right up to the front. Here Catt saw people who were finely dressed. Many of them looked like nobles or merchants or priests, mixed together with a scattering of more common looking folk. In spite of all the finery, the different kinds of styles and the bright decorations and the outlandish hats and capes made for such a riotous variety of clothing, that Catt didn't feel her plain travelling clothes made her stand out. Instead, she felt partially invisible thanks to being surrounded by other people who were trying so hard to stand out.

Lemmy found some free chairs, and they sat down. "We are just in time! The feast is always first," he explained, "then the main ceremonies, and after that the revelry goes on for much of the night. I'll certainly be too exhausted to last through all of that. I am not as young as I used to be!"

"Everything looks so good!" Catt said, focusing her attention on the dishes arrayed on the table. She observed that the serving dishes were being occasionally passed from person to person, making their way up one side of the long table, and down the other.

Someone in a white apron placed clean plates and cool moist towels in front of each of them. Catt wiped her hands clean, and began to grab food and fill her plate.

Lemmy kept his mitre on his head. Apparently local etiquette did not mandate the removal of hats while eating. Lemmy stood on the chair rather than sitting, which made it possible for him to reach his plate. Several times Catt found herself helping Lemmy with the serving dishes. Some of them were much too big and heavy for him to take and pass with his tiny arms.

"This is exquisite!" Catt proclaimed between bites. There were so many dishes that Catt realized she would have no hope of sampling everything at the table. She started taking the smallest portions she could manage in order to maximize the number of different foods she would get to taste. One leg of roast fowl, one leg of tree-lobster, one small scoop of savory herb encrusted root vegetables, a modest portion of a sweet salad that seemed to consist more of flowers than of leaves.

By the time the flow of passed dishes slowed enough for Catt to finish most of her plate, she realized that Lemmy was now leaning back in his chair, his little belly bulging.

"I fear I have indulged too much!" confessed the smiling High Priest.

"Understandable!" Catt replied with her mouth full, as she took a small glass of wine from a tray carried by a white-aproned server.

"I can never resist the rum-soaked termite jelly," said Lemmy, "even though it makes me sleepy."

"That was the blue stuff with the black bits in it, right? It was delicious!" Catt said, tipping her glass towards an azure stain in one corner of her plate.

Lemmy just nodded, a pleasant dreamy look on his face as he stared off into the crowd.

Suddenly he said, "That's the King, right over there."

Lemmy directed Catt's gaze towards a table directly in front of the huge ornate front gate of the palace. He was so close that Catt could have hit him with a poppy-seed roll if she had been inclined to throw one.

"Really!?" Catt studied the King curiously. He looked older than her, but not so very old. He had big strong-looking shoulders. He had a neatly trimmed grey beard, pointed ears, and on top of his long straight hair was a simple gold crown that looked modest and plain compared to other hats at the table. His face looked peaceful and regal, and also a little bit drunk. He was sharing his table with people who looked like diplomats and judges. Catt noted that the King passed dishes and served himself, just like everyone else, although he did seem to have a dedicated server tending only to his wine glass, which was much larger than everyone else's. There were also two black-clad people wearing masks standing close behind the King. Catt could see the blue crest on their chests which she recognized from the cop she had seen that morning. She guessed that they must be bodyguards.

"Well, cheers to the King!" Catt said. "He knows how to throw a good party." She held up her glass to Lemmy.

"Indeed! Cheers to the King!" Lemmy reached forward to retrieve his own glass from the table, and they shared a private toast to their host.

Someone a few tables down waved and said Lemmy's name. Lemmy waved back.

"I spy a good friend and fellow priest of a competing temple, I would be remiss if I did not go and pay my greetings." Lemmy said, with an apologetic tone.

"Go for it," said Catt. "I'll be fine on my own."

Lemmy climbed down from his chair, and soon all Catt could see was his giant hat, bobbing slightly and moving away through the crowd.

## Segna

Catt surveyed the table to see if there was anything she wanted more of. She felt pretty full already.

Catt watched some musicians setting up three large stringed instruments just inside the palace doors behind the King's table. The other larger band in the square was still audible.

Catt looked around to see if there was anyone interesting looking nearby for her to strike up a conversation with. The two people sitting closest to her seemed to be in the middle of an argument about the comparative merits of different types of irrigation tax subsidies.

Catt spotted a small black ant crawling on the tabletop. It quested back and forth as if searching. Catt took a sticky crumb off her plate and dropped it in the ant's path. The tiny creature reared up on four legs to inspect the morsel.

Catt thought about the goddess Lemmy had recommended. Crawling things, and rotting food.

The ant picked up the crumb and began to carry it away in the opposite direction.

"Do you want your name included in the Lots?"

Catt looked up. A person in a white uniform was standing there holding a metal bowl and an ornate box with a slot in the top.

"Lots?" Catt asked, wondering if it was some kind of raffle.

"Yes. Do you want your name included?" The man spoke with a note of disdain in his voice which Catt interpreted to mean that he was expected to ask this question to everyone, but wished he could skip past her.

"Yeah... Sure I want to."

The man gave her a small round flat token and a quill pen.

Catt couldn't tell if the token was made from very smooth wood, or if it was some sort of large seed. She signed "Catt Zago" on one side.

"Both sides" said the man.

Catt didn't like his tone, so she flipped the token over and signed again very slowly, taking delicate care with the loops of each letter.

When she was finished the man held out the box, and Catt dropped the token into the slot.

"Hope I win!" she said.

"As do I," said the man with a roll of his eyes. He moved on down the table to interrupt the pair who were arguing about water tax policy. "Do either of you wish to have your names in the Lots?"

Catt was about to rise and go explore what else the festival might have to offer, when a voice asked, "Is this seat taken?"

Catt looked and her heart fluttered in her chest as she saw a stunningly beautiful woman with one hand resting on the back of the chair that Lemmy had vacated.

She had piercing orange eyes and full lips. Her hair was shaved smooth. She was wearing a loose skirt and top of beige material decorated with patterns of bright turquoise rectangles. Tattooed scripts laced her bare collarbones and midriff in a shade that would have been almost invisible on her dark skin if not for the fact that it reflected the light of the setting sun differently.

For an instant, Catt was paralyzed, but then she swept Lemmy's plate out of the way with her arm, and pulled out the chair for the woman. "It's all yours!" said Catt.

"Thank you," said the woman, sitting.

Catt turned her eyes back to her plate, trying not to stare at the newcomer's supple curves.

Catt felt a wave of self doubt, wondering what she could say to make conversation.

"Did you put your name in the Lots?" Catt asked suddenly.

"No... I usually don't participate," said the woman, looking over the remaining dishes of food.

"What's the matter?" Catt said teasingly. "Afraid you might win?"

The woman stared into the distance and answered thoughtfully, "No, I suppose I am not afraid. I could handle winning."

"Well, you can't win if you don't play!" said Catt.

Catt whistled for the man with the Lots box. "Hey, the lady here didn't get a chance!"

The man looked a little annoyed, but he returned and offered the pen and a token to the woman.

Catt watched her sign, but couldn't read her name.

The woman dropped her token into the box. "There, it's done."

The man with the box moved away, pointedly avoiding looking at Catt.

"What's your name?" Catt asked.

"I am called Segna Ur-Segna," the woman said, turning her eyes to meet Catt's. "Who are you?"

Catt grinned, "My name's Catt Zago."

"Most pleased to make your acquaintance, Catt Zago," Segna said.

"I like your tattoos," said Catt. "What do they say?"

Segna glanced down. "This? It is a verse from my favorite magic spell."

"I can't read it, but it is beautiful," said Catt.

"Thank you," said Segna.

"Do you have any other verses on you?" Catt asked.

Segna looked Catt in the eye, "You are very forward, Catt Zago."

Knots of anxiety tangled with churning butterflies of hope in Catt's stomach.

"I find it saves time…" Catt said, holding eye contact. "I can stop being forward if you don't like it."

Segna quirked her lovely eyebrow. "No, you don't have to stop right now," Segna said.

Catt felt giddy, but forced herself to remain cool.

"So, magic spells?" Catt asked, "Are you a magician? Or do you just appreciate them as body art?"

Segna smiled. "I teach magic at the University of Bakak."

"Oh!" Catt grinned, "That's the wizard school! You must be very good then! Can you do a fireball right here?"

Segna laughed. To Catt it seemed musical. "I am *very* good," said Segna, "but no, I cannot 'do a fireball' here, I doubt anyone is that good."

"Why?" Catt asked, genuinely curious. She didn't know much about magic, but she understood small fireballs to be entry-level wizarding stuff.

Segna looked at Catt, puzzlement on her face. "The Unburning… are… do you not know about that?"

Catt suddenly felt like the outsider that she was. Her facade of confidence was cracked. "No, I don't know what that is," she admitted.

"You must have just ridden in with this morning's caravan!" exclaimed Segna.

The words weren't said unkindly, but Catt felt her cheeks flush with embarrassment at being so transparently identified as a foreigner.

"I..." Catt didn't know what to say next.

As if understanding Catt's discomfort, Segna's expression softened, and she placed a hand on Catt's arm. "Don't worry about it," she soothed. "The Unburning is an old magic curse. No fire can burn in the city. It is very strange, and very boring, and everyone gets used to it and ignores it."

Catt barely heard Segna's explanation. She was just thinking about the softness of the hand on her arm.

Segna changed the subject. "What about you, Catt? Tell me about yourself and where you are from."

Catt wasn't sure she wanted to talk about herself yet, and she definitely didn't want to talk about where she was from, so she changed the subject again. "You must be hungry," Catt suggested.

"I am actually," said Segna, "I seem to have arrived too late."

Most people at the table had already finished eating, and the circular flow of serving dishes had all but stopped.

"Wait here!" said Catt, and she leaped up and moved from table to table grabbing dishes, returning to Segna a moment later with her arms precariously laden with half empty dishes of delicacies.

She arrayed the dishes on the table in front of Segna, and apologized, "I'm sorry I couldn't find any clean plates, but I don't think anyone will mind."

Segna smiled demurely, and picked a small skewer of little pieces of roast meat from one of the serving dishes. "Thank you, Catt," she said.

"How long have you been teaching magic?" asked Catt, wanting to keep the conversation going.

Segna finished swallowing a bite, and said, "Not for nearly as long as I have been studying magic. I've only been teaching for three years, but it feels like I have been at the university forever." Before Catt could stop her, Segna turned the questioning around, "What do you do, Catt?"

This was more comfortable territory than "Where are you from?" but Catt still wanted to choose her words carefully. She shoved a morsel from a random dish into her mouth to buy herself an instant to collect her thoughts.

Catt decided that she wanted to be honest, yet vague. "Oh, mostly people pay me to stop trouble, or to start it."

"How mercenary!" said Segna, but she was hiding a smile.

Catt grinned unashamedly. "But really I aspire to stop and start trouble on my own terms... you know, be my own boss."

"An entrepreneur of trouble?" suggested Segna with a twinkle in her eye and a cold pastry-puff hovering in her fingers near her lips.

"I do like trouble," Catt said. And then, softly and earnestly she added, "I like you, Segna."

Segna thoughtfully ate the pastry while Catt's heart thumped.

Then Segna blinked both her eyes slowly at Catt, and whispered suggestively, "Let's not rush. We have plenty of time for trouble."

Suddenly the air was full of a low thrumming note. It took Catt a moment to realize it was a real sound, and not her imagination.

Segna suddenly looked away, and said, "It is starting." Her voice had lost the personal and intimate tone it had carried just an instant before.

Catt looked in the direction that Segna was looking. Everyone around them was falling silent and all turning their heads in the same direction. The whole festival had become a tableau focused on one point.

The King was slumped face first in his plate. His oversized wine glass was overturned on the table next to him, one hand still half gripping it.

Behind the King, stood the two masked black-clad bodyguards. Behind them a musician was relentlessly and fluidly drawing an enormous bow across the largest of the string instruments. This was the source of the noise. Beside him stood two other musicians, frozen like statues, bows hovering ready over the other two stringed instruments.

From this central noise, Catt could hear the silence spreading. The distant orchestra fell quiet, and it felt like the whole festival, the whole square, the whole city was holding its breath as this one mad musician played this one endless throbbing note.

The two bodyguards finally moved, simultaneously climbing over the table on either side of the King as if the table was just a stepping stone.

One of them put his hand to the King's neck. He nodded to the other.

The other bodyguard reached to his belt and drew out a black hand-axe with a short handle and an enormous gleaming blade.

"The King is Dead!" shouted the first bodyguard, removing his hand from the King's neck.

The one with the axe slowly raised the weapon high up above his head.

It was at this instant that Catt realized that the black-clad men were not bodyguards, they were something else. She jumped up from her chair in a panic, one hand going reflexively to the hilt of her sword.

Segna's soft hands grabbed Catt with iron strength and dragged Catt back down into her seat. "Don't stand while the King is dying!" Segna whispered sharply. Catt could feel Segna's breath right in her ear.

Catt turned to Segna and protested, "But they are killing–"

Segna interrupted Catt by placing two fingers over Catt's lips.

"Also don't speak while the King is dying," whispered Segna, more gently now.

Nobody around them heard this exchange because at the same moment, the other two musicians acted upon some cue and began furiously carving a melody from their instruments. The first deep note was still there, and now added to it was a frenetic sorrowfully refrain that seemed to be entirely composed of tones and timbres calculated to tug at one's emotional core.

The axe fell with the swiftness of a hawk diving on prey. Catt flinched as it bit deep into the back of the King's neck.

Segna squeezed both of Catt's hands under the table.

The axe rose and fell twice more, finally striking the table as the King's head rolled forward close to the edge, but not falling off.

The music of the stringed instruments raged on. Nobody moved.

Catt became aware that she was fighting back tears. It wasn't the violence. Catt had seen violence before– done violence before. The emotion that was overwhelming her came from the sense of being out of her element, from the juxtaposition of this deadly ritual in the middle of a peaceful festival, and from the surreal calm of the total stranger she had been flirting with a moment before, who was now comforting her and at the same time behaving as if this was all normal.

The executioner with the axe hung the bloodied weapon back on his belt, and gingerly picked up the King's crown.

Catt was determined not to cry. She focused on her breathing, and squeezed Segna's hands back.

The other black-clad executioner took a golden rod from his coat. He spoke a word of command, and the wand hummed. "**Reveal Enchantments?**" asked a strange voice that must have been coming from the wand itself.

The executioner spoke a word of confirmation, and waved it slowly back and forth over the King's corpse. The rod glowed with a white light, and then the King's remains glowed with the same white light.

After a few seconds, both lights faded away. The executioner with the rod shouted, "We have verified that the body is free from enchantments of illusion, transmutation, and necromancy!"

The executioner with the crown shouted, "The King is Dead! Let the Lots Begin!" and as he said this he took a black cloth out from somewhere and unfurled it, and spread it over the dead King. He then placed the crown on top of the now-concealed lump that had been the late King's head.

Segna whispered to Catt, "The worst is over!"

A tiny laugh escaped Catt's mouth. It was a release of tension.

The two executioners stepped aside.

From somewhere, deep drum-beats joined the stringed instruments.

Four dancers ran in from somewhere, Catt had not seen them approaching. The dancers converged in the space in front of the King's table. One of them had a large square cloth with an intricate two-color pattern on it. Each dancer grabbed a corner of the cloth and they stretched it between them. They whirled and rotated and gyrated.

The silence of the crowd was broken and now a ripple of voices and laughter and cheers mixed with the music.

Catt's muscles began to relax. She had just witnessed a ritual king-killing, but it was all part of the show. It was all part of the festival. Her shoulder was pressed against Segna's. Catt could feel her warmth.

A line of white-clad people approached the four dancers. Each of them was bearing an ornate box. The dancers slowed but the drum-beats intensified. Each white-clad box-bearer emptied their box onto the cloth that was now spread tight between the four dancers.

By the time the last box had been emptied, the cloth was stretched down under the weight of the small coin-like objects.

They were tokens, each with a name written on the front and the back. As Catt realized what they were, she also realized in a distant detached way that her own name was there in that pile somewhere.

The dancers began to circle again. Every few beats of the drum they would pull the cloth taut and lift, flinging the mass of tokens into the air, and catching them again.

Each time the tokens were thrown up, some of them failed to land on the cloth, raining down instead on the ground, on the dancers, on the nearby tables, on the heads of onlookers, on the black cloth that covered the King's body.

The pile dwindled, and the dancers moved gracefully with their feet sliding across the ground, sliding and displacing swaths of fallen tokens as they went.

Soon there were only a handful of tokens remaining. There was excitement in the crowd. People were clapping along with the drums now. The festival felt like a festival again.

Catt felt giddy with the awareness that she and Segna were still holding hands under the table. She didn't dare move. She didn't want to let go.

With a final flourish of music, the dancers lowered the cloth to the ground. Three of them knelt and became motionless as statues. One straightened up. The crowd roared and cheered.

The standing dancer stepped forward to the center of the cloth, bowed, and picked up the last remaining token.

One of the masked executioners, still standing off to the side shouted in a booming voice, "The Royal Lots Have Been Cast!"

The crowd's roar crescendoed, and then gradually fell silent.

The dancer was looking at the token. They lifted it high over their head, and announced;

"Segna Ur-Segna!"

The three other dancers repeated in powerful voices, "Segna Ur-Segna! The new King's name is Segna Ur-Segna!"

# Coronation

Segna rose. She felt as if this was a dream. She began walking around the table towards the coronation dancers.

The crowd was cheering and singing her name. People were jumping up on their chairs, and flinging their hats into the air.

As she was almost to the coronation cloth, Segna glanced back to look for Catt Zago, that strange brash flirtatious woman whose advances she had been entertaining. She was no longer visible among the throngs of brightly-dressed revelers and falling hats. Segna felt a twinge of regret at not having said something, but when her name was called, she had moved as if in a trance.

Like so many people who had grown up in Great Bakak, Segna had imagined many times what it might feel like to be chosen in the Royal Lots. She had fantasized about what sort of things she would do with the power of the kingship, and she had pondered whether she would be brave enough to face the inevitable axe at the end of that one glorious year.

Segna's sandals were treading on fallen tokens with other people's names written on them. Any adult could enter. Anyone could become King. Segna could remember the first time she had entered. She could remember the first festival in which her guardians had grudgingly permitted her to drop her token into the box along with theirs. She also remembered how relieved they had been when a stranger's name was called, and how disappointed she herself had been that first time. That was more than half a lifetime away now.

Segna stepped into the coronation cloth, and stood in its center, arms outstretched slightly, looking up to the mountains, and up to the darkening sky. She had seen this ceremony so many times before, she knew how she was expected to act.

Now the primary coronation dancer pressed the token into her hand. Segna lifted it to her eyes. This was the point of no return. This was the point where she could open her mouth and say "No, this is not my name", or "Someone forged my name, this is not my handwriting."

If she denied her name, no questions would be asked. No graphologist would be called to examine her penstrokes. The fallen tokens would simply be gathered up, scraped into a pile on the coronation cloth, and the Dance of Royal Lots would begin all over again, with her own name excluded.

She had seen this happen before. Anyone could become King, but noone would be forced to take on the deadly mantle of power against their own will. She also knew that the crowd would love it if she refused. The second dance was always far more suspenseful than the first, but did she want to refuse? Or did she want to accept, and allow her life to be magnificently changed... for a price?

She could see her own neat handwriting on the token. She could see her own name. The rest of the festival– the rest of the world– became a blur of light and color and noise. Why had she even entered her name in the Lots? It had been so long. Back when she had first devoted herself to the study of magic, she had stopped playing the Lots. She still came to the Festival for the food and the spectacle and the dancing, but she had lost interest in playing the game of who might become King. Why had she played tonight?

As she pondered in this instant what she should do, her mouth seemed to decide for her. "I am Segna Ur-Segna, I accept the Royal Lot!"

The crowd roared.

Segna remembered later the feeling of the cold crown being placed on her bare head. She remembered the twirling of the coronation dancers making her dizzy. She remembered a feeling of elation looking at the expressions of joy on the faces of celebrating strangers.

She remembered walking up the steps of the palace– *her* palace now. She remembered being introduced to advisors, but she didn't remember any of their names. She remembered being told that "no" she could not go home to get her things, because she was already home, and servants could be dispatched to bring her anything she needed. She remembered being given the finest wine she had ever tasted. She remembered looking out a high window at the festival. Tables had been moved away and people were dancing in the square now, celebrating her coronation, celebrating the beginning of the new year.

Segna fell asleep in the middle of a huge and luxurious and unfamiliar bed, head spinning, heart delirious, memory clouded, daydreams and wishes fulfilled, fear and doubt forgotten, and future sealed with blood.

# Remains

As the winner of the Royal Lots approached the coronation cloth, Senior Executioner Crocken tapped his partner on the shoulder.

"Let's go," Crocken growled. "She doesn't need to be looking at us right now."

He and Jantos moved towards the palace, skirting around the musicians. They took up station in the shadows of one of the huge ornate columns that decorated the front of the building. Here they would be out of sight, out of mind, but still close enough to listen, and to keep an eye on the rapidly cooling body of the old king.

Senior Executioner Jantos immediately sat down and took out a black cloth and began cleaning the royal blood off his axe. "Three damn strikes, I should have done it in one," Jantos berated himself.

Crocken ignored his partner and watched the coronation. He was listening to see whether or not the new King would accept her Lot. If she denied it, he was going to have to go back down there and shout his lines again to formally re-start the dance.

She seemed to make up her mind relatively quickly, and accepted, so Crocken relaxed. He scratched his beard underneath the mask.

Jantos was still complaining. "Wouldn't've happened if my aim had been better... blasted vertebrae!"

"You did fine, Jant," Crocken reassured.

"It wasn't how I wanted it to be," Jantos fussed. He glanced up from his axe, yellow eyes flashing through his eyeholes. "I wanted one clean smooth chop. Bam! Fin!"

"You were plenty clean," Crocken pointed out, "Same cut, all three times. I saw. That was skill."

"Pah!" Jantos protested, "It don't matter how accurate the second and third one was if the first strike was sloppy. I'm not gonna get another go at it. Killing a King is a once-in-a lifetime chance."

Crocken snorted, and turned his attention back to watching the crowd.

"You get to wave the wand and say the lines every time," Jantos persisted, "but the Reaper picks a new axe-man every year. That was my one shot, and I blew it."

Crocken didn't bother saying that four years wasn't "every time", he just tried to ignore his partner.

Crocken could see the outline of the dead king under his cloth clearly. The people sitting closest to the old king had cleared away as soon as the ceremony had started, and now that people were up and dancing for the new King, the old king's table was completely empty.

Jantos fell quiet, and put away his now-gleaming axe.

They both waited in silence until the new King was led into the palace by the royal advisers.

"Right then," Jantos said with a sigh, "I'll fetch the clean-up crew. I want to get this done, unmask, and go have a drink."

"Make sure you don't complain about work unmasked," advised Crocken.

Jantos glared back angrily for a moment, then his shoulders slumped. "You're right. I'll drink at home tonight," he conceded.

Crocken watched Jantos walk away. He resumed watching the motionless lump under the black cloth. He didn't feel bad for the dead king. He didn't feel pity for the new King. Dying was just part of what a King was. Some of the other guild executioners had high ideals about what the Regicide meant. They would say it was their duty to continually purge corruption from power. They would say that the certainty of the axe would focus the King on the higher purpose of governing well and creating a legacy. Crocken wasn't so sure about any of that. He thought it was just a tradition. A particularly visceral and emotional way to put the past year to rest, and let people hope that the new year would be better.

After a while, he saw Jantos return leading four junior executioners. The juniors had a stretcher. They loaded the shrouded king onto the stretcher, while Jantos made sure the head was secure. Crocken noticed when Jantos discreetly examined the neck.

Most of the people celebrating the festival had moved off. Now that the new King had gone into her palace, the focus of the festival had shifted to the orchestra and people were dancing below the terrace, under the trees in the square. Still, a few people were always more interested in death. A small procession of curious folk formed behind Jantos and the Juniors as they carried away the old king towards his appointed undertaker's office.

Crocken checked the wand, and then exited the square himself by a different route.

The dark streets were largely quiet. Every now and then, music and laughter would pour out of an open window where some people might be celebrating the new year in their own way, but for the most part the city was quiet. The usual night life was concentrated into the festival.

Crocken reflected that it would probably be a big night for stealth burglaries. He would be dealing with that aftermath tomorrow. Actual executions were a relatively small part of the responsibilities of the Guild of Executioners, and most of the rest of the time they were expected to make themselves useful by assisting the courts and the kingship with the enforcement of laws and the investigation of crimes. Routine policework was most of the job, and it was only so very rarely that an executioner got to wave the magic wand to prove that a freshly decapitated king wasn't a trick or an illusion.

The wand had to be returned back to the guild headquarters before midnight. That was the rule. Crocken picked up his pace even though he knew he still had plenty of time. The Reaper had no patience for tardiness.

# Reaper

The Reaper sat motionless in a wooden chair in the armory of the guild-hall. The walls were covered with row upon row of axes. Alcoves contained tools for sharpening and repairing.

One small magic lamp simply illuminated the area with a dull green luminescence.

The Reaper was waiting for Senior Executioner Crocken– or more precisely, the item he would be carrying.

After a long silent while, the lock turned and the door opened.

The masked person that the Reaper recognized as Crocken squinted into the gloom around the lamp for a while.

"Oh! There you are, Sir!" Crocken said when his eyes had adjusted enough to spot the Reaper.

"There I am." The Reaper did not stand.

Crocken approached, took the wand out of his coat, and offered it.

The Reaper took it. "The King?"

"The King died very well," said Crocken. "Jantos did a good job. Very clean." Crocken shifted his weight from one foot to the other.

"The wand?" asked the Reaper.

"No magic detected," Crocken confirmed, "everything went normally. The Lots also went well. The new King accepted on the first round."

The Reaper inclined their head slightly, in acknowledgement that Crocken had correctly anticipated the question.

A moment of dead silence hung between them.

"Well... If that's all Sir, I'll be going," Crocken said.

"Yes," the Reaper nodded.

Crocken backed towards the door. "Have a good New Year Sir," he said, flinching with embarrassment at his own words before the sentence was completely out of his mouth.

The Reaper looked at the Senior Executioner. The Reaper understood Crocken. He required encouragement. "You have done well. Go."

Crocken looked relieved. He closed the door behind him, and the lock clicked.

Crocken was a very good executioner, but there was a fundamental difference between the Senior Executioner and the Reaper. Crocken was the sort of man who would go home and take his mask off and become a person again, and then go to bed and sleep until it was time to wake up and put the mask on again.

Finally the Reaper rose from the chair, and carrying the wand, walked through the armory. Past the shelves of wooden masks, for every shape and size of face. Past the racks full of the more specialized weapons, for the situations when an axe was not enough. Past the sealed cabinets of things too useful to destroy after being confiscated from the dead. Past the special glass cabinet where the wand would wait for the remainder of the year until it was needed for the next Regicide Festival.

There was somewhere the wand needed to be taken before it could be put away. There was something that needed to be done with it before it could be locked in that cabinet.

The Reaper opened the secret door, and took the wand down the pitch black spiral stair.

# Summons

Five days had passed since the Regicide Feast. Lemmy had been very busy. Most religions had their own calendars that started at different times, but still, enough of them were synchronized with the city's official calendar that the first few days of the year tended to be a very active time for someone in the priest-of-all-gods trade.

When a messenger stopped by the Polypantheonic Temple that morning bearing a terse note requesting his immediate presence at the High Courthouse, Lemmy presumed that it was probably a wedding or an annulment for a worshiper of some obscure deity, and that the officiant had failed to adequately prepare, and therefore urgently needed to consult with Lemmy's considerable font of experience. That sort of thing had happened before.

He continued with his appointments, but when he found a gap in his schedule after a goat's milk baptism, he washed up, flipped the sign in the window, tacked a "Back Soon" note to his temple door, and hurried off to Court.

# Sandwiches

Catt Zago was having a very bad time. She remembered getting very drunk at the festival, and arguing angrily with various people about whether or not it was okay to behead beautiful Kings. An infuriating number of them had supported the position that it was fine. It must have come to fist-fighting at some point, but she couldn't quite remember that part clearly.

After waking up in the small cell, and waiting for the hangover to wear off, she was moderately proud to note that the bruises on her knuckles felt much worse than the ones on her face, so she had probably fought relatively well.

Catt had on a few occasions in her life gained a little knowledge of prisons, so she knew enough to have recognized immediately that this was an unusual one, and she had been left with several full days to worry about that.

It was dark like a dungeon, and though she could see a few other cells, she had seen no other prisoners, and she had only distantly heard sounds that *might* have been other prisoners. However, unlike a dungeon, the cell was quite clean, and contained a perfectly comfortable cot with an actual pillow and blanket, both completely free of vermin.

Three times a day, a guard would arrive, carrying a narrow tray with a fresh cold sandwich and a clay cup of water. This would be wordlessly placed outside the bars, and if she had pushed the old tray and cup out between the bars, the guard would carry it away. They didn't seem to particularly care if she kept the tray and cup either. Once Catt had realized this, she had accumulated a fine collection of eight clay cups.

Once per day, a guard would arrive with a very narrow chamber pot, and slide it between the bars in exchange for the old one, which they would then carry away. The chamber pots had tight fitting lids to contain the smell, but Catt had refrained from discovering whether or not they would allow her to hoard them.

This dungeon was actually more luxurious than many boarding houses that Catt had occasioned to visit, but it was still clearly a dungeon. There were strong metal bars blocking the exit, and she was not able to leave.

This was all very concerning. It was a highly unusual way to treat a prisoner, particularly one who had apparently only been picked up for drunk and disorderly fighting.

What really had Catt frightened was the guards themselves. Every single one of them was an executioner. They all wore the same black caped uniform and wooden face mask as the two kingslayers had worn. They all had the same blue badge with an axe over a crown that she had seen before. Its meaning was painfully obvious to her now in hindsight. And of course they each wore a sharp-looking axe on their belt.

None of the executioner-guards ever spoke a single word to her. They just delivered sandwiches or chamberpots and then departed again. As far as she could tell, it had been a different executioner every time. The wooden mask was always the same, but the hair and neck and arms and general body shape of the executioners was widely varied. Some were women, some were men. A few had tails.

What sort of a city could she be in, that would have so many king-slayers that some of them would spend their time delivering tasty sandwiches to drunkards in dungeons?

After much pondering, Catt had come to the conclusion that she would be killed soon. It was the only explanation that made any sense. If every crime carried the death sentence, then perhaps the city could afford to keep prisoners in such lavish conditions inside such a clean prison. After all, if every prisoner was to be promptly beheaded, there would be no overcrowding, and no repeat-offenders. It was just her luck to have stumbled unaware into a city under the draconian heel of some kind of murderous death-cult.

By now Catt reckoned it had been a bit more than four days, and she was certain that each sandwich would be her last meal. What kind of monsters gave their captives sliced tomatoes and aged cheese anyways? She spent her idle time alternating between doing push-ups on the floor, and sprawling on the cot trying to imagine ways to fight back when the inevitable time came.

She determined that she could start by pelting them with the clay cups, and that perhaps she could somehow wield either the chamberpot or the bed as a weapon. Ultimately though, all her escape fantasies came down to wrestling the axe away from one of them and fighting her way out. It was a doomed plan of course– there were far too many of the masked bastards for that approach to have a prayer of working. At best, she might manage to take a few of them with her before they cut her down, and as far as escape fantasies go, that one was... Unsatisfying.

# Release

The next executioner to peer through the bars at her was empty-handed.

Catt tensed and she reached slowly and smoothly for the pyramid of cups.

Not entirely empty-handed. A key-ring jingled in the executioner's hand as they began to unlock the door.

As Catt got a clear look at her executioner, her heart sank, and the clay cup dropped harmless out of her fingers.

This one was so huge, they had to turn their shoulders sideways to fit through the cell door. Massively muscled arms protruded from the black uniform, with skin the texture of red sandstone. The keyring was held daintily in hands bigger than Catt's head, with fingers each ending in hooked claws. The ogre's face was too big to be completely covered by the mask, and she could see where the eye-holes had been whittled larger to accommodate widely-set eyes. This executioner's axe seemed to be twice the size of the other ones she had seen.

Catt sat up straight on the cot, swallowed, and waited for her life to flash before her eyes.

"Good news, miss! You're to be released!" said the ogre, cheerfully.

# Judge

"Speak politely to the Judge, and you'll be just fine, miss," advised the huge executioner as Catt was led up a flight of stairs to a well-lit hallway. "It'll be the third door on the right."

Catt took a few uncertain steps down the hall. She was completely unbound. No chains, no manacles. Sunlight was streaming into the door-lined hallway from an open window at the far end.

Catt glanced back at the executioner.

The massive ogre inclined its masked head slightly, and waved a clawed hand. "Best of luck!" the ogre said, and then turned and retreated down the stairs.

Catt stood alone in the hallway for what felt like quite some time. She stared out the open window, but after a while she finally determined that she would chance the third door on the right.

Through the door was a room with several rows of empty seats facing a big desk. At the desk was an old man wearing a large white wig. He had a single eye directly in the middle of his face. It was currently cast downward at a book in his hands, but it swiveled up to look at Catt as she cautiously approached.

"Ah, Catt Zago," he drawled, wrinkled jowls jiggling as he spoke.

"Yes?" Catt was not sure exactly what she was supposed to do. She guessed this was the Judge, and she was relieved that he was not dressed like an executioner. She could see her pack resting open on the corner of the desk.

"You stand accused of one charge of Public Nuisancery, Three Counts of Battery by Fisticuffs, one count of Drunkenness While in Possession of an Unlicensed Sword, and one count of Insulting the King In The Presence Of An Officer Of The Law."

Catt decided it was best to say nothing for now.

The Judge continued. "Where are your accusers?" He rolled his eye, looking around the empty courtroom.

Catt looked too, and was startled to realize that one of the seats in the front row was not empty. High Priest Lemmy was sitting there.

Lemmy said nothing, he just smiled at her.

"I... um..." Catt stammered.

"Right," said the Judge, "The court finds no accusers in attendance. The charges of Nuicancery and Fisticuffs are hereby dropped for lack of evidence."

Catt's mouth hung open for an instant, and then she managed to say, "Thank you?"

The Judge glared at her seriously. "As for the matter of the unlicensed sword, the court hereby declares that the weapon will be permanently confiscated, and that you, Catt Zago will be ineligible for a sword license during the term of your probationary period, pending a positive report from your intercessor."

"My intercessor?"

"Yes, your spiritual advisor has agreed to act as intercessor for your case." The Judge smiled and nodded towards where Lemmy was sitting.

"Indeed!" confirmed Lemmy.

"May I just add, as a personal aside," said the Judge in a confidential tone, "How very fortunate you are that the High Priest was willing to vouch for you! Normally a family member would act as intercessor, and as we weren't able to locate one for you, it's lucky for you we found his name in your possessions."

The Judge waggled the book he was holding, and Catt realized it was the same book that Lemmy had given her the first time she had met him.

The Judge cleared his throat, "And finally, the charge of Insulting the King."

He put the book down on top of Catt's pack, and picked up a thin sheaf of a few papers from the desk.

"I have carefully reviewed the report from the arresting executioner, and I must say, although these words betray an inappropriately... *familiar* attitude towards the King, I dare say I am hard-pressed to interpret them as insults."

Catt bit her lip. She had no memory of what she might have said, and she didn't dare to ask.

"Do you have anything to say in your own defense?" the Judge asked.

"Mmm.... I'm sorry?" Catt hazarded, "It won't happen again?"

"See that it doesn't," said the Judge sternly. "I am reducing the last charge to a Warning Of Reprimand." Then the Judge turned his attention to Lemmy. "Now. High Priest Lemmy of the Polypantheonic Temple..."

Lemmy stood on his chair. "Yes, your honor."

"Do you affirm, as discussed earlier, to act as court-appointed intercessor for the criminal Catt Zago, and to make reasonable effort to re-integrate her into the lawful society of Great Bakak?"

"I so affirm," said Lemmy seriously.

"In that case," said the Judge, "Catt Zago, I release you into your own custody."

"Thank y–" Catt began.

"And finally, we must settle the bill for your sojourn with us." The Judge held up a small ledger. "That was five nights of lodging, and fourteen meals, plus the cleaning surcharge, that comes to six Shmouds and five Thorbs."

"Ah..." said Catt, mentally putting the sandwiches into context.

"The Court took the liberty of having your foreign gold coins converted into Shmouds, and we have already deducted your expenses, so your account with the prison can be closed immediately. Here is your change." The Judge placed three small silver coins and one tiny copper coin on the desk next to Catt's bag.

Catt stared at the paltry-looking coins. She had already known that her gold was gone, but until now she had assumed that someone had taken it after the drunken fight. Her surprise at getting a fraction of it back was stifled by her realization that she had most certainly been robbed by means of a poor exchange rate and an inflated bill. Somehow that was worse than a mugging.

Catt composed herself, swept up the bag and the coins, and backed away from the desk. She knew she should probably say something polite to the Judge, thank him for his mercy or something, but she didn't *want* to.

"Thank you, your honor, may all the gods bless you," said Lemmy, hopping down from the chair and bowing low to the Judge, and turning to go.

When Catt realized Lemmy was heading for the door, Catt led the way, and in a moment they were back in the hall.

# Intuition

Exiting the courthouse, Catt found herself again in the square. There were the rows of trees, there was the raised terrace, there was the palace with the mountains behind it. It looked very different than it had the night of the festival. It was all wide empty spaces, and smooth stone surfaces shining in the sun. There were relatively few people moving about in the large space, and all of them were either finely dressed like ladies and lords, or else in various professional uniforms, white robes, clerical vestments, messenger's livery, or black garb and wooden masks.

Catt cringed at the sight of executioners standing around as if they were the city watch... which, she was realizing, is exactly what they seemed to be.

"Would you care to walk with me?" asked Lemmy.

"Sure," said Catt tersely, eager to leave the square.

They walked in silence for a while, out of the square, away from the temples and official buildings, and into streets that were lined with shops and filled with people who were dressed a little bit more commonly.

"Why didn't you tell me they were going to kill him!?" Catt said, abruptly wheeling on the tiny priest.

Confusion clouded Lemmy's face for only an instant. "Ah, yes, the Regicide. I am sorry. It occurred to me too late that I should have explained it, but by then it had already happened, and I didn't know where you had gotten to."

"Chopping a King's head off during the dessert course is a big thing to forget about!" Catt shouted.

"In my opinion it is the low of the evening, while the meal is the high point." Lemmy said.

Catt gritted her teeth and then hissed angrily, "What about the part where they pick who to kill next year, and she just walks up there and agrees to it?"

Lemmy remained silent.

"Is everyone here okay with killing kings?" She demanded, and then a little louder, "Am I just crazy? Doesn't anybody else care that the guys with the axes are obviously actually running this city?"

"Is this lady bothering you, Reverend Lemmy?" asked a burly woman who was passing by. Her chainmail clinked as she put a gauntleted fist to her hip and glared at Catt.

"Not at all, Ms Inglaron," Lemmy soothed. "My dear friend Ms Zago and I are merely debating politics."

"Oh," said the woman, seemingly mollified by this. "All right then. Be well, Reverend."

"Be well, Ms Inglaron," replied Lemmy. "May Sirth's light and strength bolster you!"

The woman walked away.

Catt stared at Lemmy, trying to fathom whether he had been sincere or facetious in describing her as a "friend".

"Why did you help me out of prison?" Catt changed the subject.

"I was concerned for your well-being."

"That's it?" asked Catt. "Does this mean I owe you something now?"

"Not in the least," said Lemmy, "on the contrary, I believe I owe you further assistance."

Catt narrowed her eyes. "That's the 'intercessor' thing?"

Lemmy shrugged. "Partly, yes."

"And what else?" asked Catt.

"Well..." said Lemmy slowly, "also I simply had an intuition. When I heard about your predicament, I felt it was important not to turn my back on you."

"Why?"

"My dear Ms Zago, I worship nearly every god that I know about. I have learned to follow intuition when I feel it."

"Huh." Catt made a non-committal noise, and then asked, "So, what now? You planning on following me around to make sure I don't get into any more drunken fights?"

Lemmy chuckled. "Not in the least. In fact I must hurry back to the temple soon, I have an appointment to conduct a naming ceremony to dedicate a newborn to the river goddess Tamathe."

"Is there a river around here?" Catt wondered aloud.

Lemmy shook his head. "No... Ms Zago, do you want a job?"

Catt was surprised. "What do you mean?" she asked.

"I have been considering for some time the possibility of hiring an acolyte," explained Lemmy. "I'm proud of the work I do, and I am proud of what the Polypantheonic Temple provides to the city, but I am just one person, and it is very hard to keep up with demand. I need help from someone resourceful, creative, and capable."

Catt looked at the priest's earnest face. She *did* think of herself as being resourceful, creative and capable, but she wondered why he would assume her to be those things.

"Maybe..." Catt replied after a moment.

# River

An hour later, Catt was an acolyte. She didn't feel any different, and she wasn't dressed any different, but she was carrying a long wooden plank over one shoulder, and following the tiny face of a sleeping baby through the streets of the city.

The baby was swaddled into a sling on its father's back. The baby was so young that its face still had a wrinkled look to it. The baby's tiny eyelids were shut, but every so often they would open and Catt would catch a glimpse of shiny black eyes. Tiny fists protruded from the swaddle, and occasionally grasped the air. On the top of the baby's nearly-bald head was the faintest wisp of green hair.

Both of the parents also had green hair, long, and each braided in a different way. They were small people, but not as small as Lemmy, who was leading the way wearing his enormous mitre.

As they walked, Lemmy sang a wordless tune of humms and trills. Catt had no idea if it was part of the ceremony or not.

They passed out of the district with its narrow shop-lined streets and stacked apartments, and towards the west part of the city where the streets grew wider, and the style of the buildings changed. Many of the structures lining the streets looked like what Catt would describe as "farm houses" except that they were too close together to be any such thing. The houses looked old, but well maintained, with fresh paint on weathered wooden walls, and cracked bricks patched neatly with mortar.

Catt shifted the plank to her other shoulder. It wasn't terribly heavy, but it wasn't light either. Catt wondered how Lemmy would have moved it before hiring her.

There were also some splashes of green here. Some of the houses had small gardens in front of them, full of unidentifiable sprouts and creeping vines and sun-catching leaves.

The street began to slope gently upwards. The houses were left behind, and terraces of actual farmland opened up around them.

They came to a brick-lined irrigation channel that ran under the road. Lemmy stopped, and the mother gently unfastened the infant from the father's back. It seemed to still be sleeping.

Lemmy indicated to Catt where to put the plank. Catt walked parallel to the irrigation trench, walking carefully so as not to tread on the small bean plants in the field. Dark water rushed in the trench. She could feel a hint of cool moisture in the air, refreshing after the general dryness of the city.

The trench looked narrow enough that Catt thought she could leap over it, if she got a running start. It also seemed deep enough, and the water running fast enough that jumping across would be something she would think twice about before attempting.

As Lemmy had instructed, she laid the plank across the trench, so it formed a bridge. She adjusted the end so it fit as flush as possible against the bricks with no wobbling.

Lemmy came up behind her. He was carrying the baby now. The parents were on the other side of the trench, and they took up positions at the far end of the plank.

Lemmy held up the baby above his head, and spoke a prayer in a language Catt didn't recognize. The baby woke up partway through and began a soft mewling cry. The parents clasped each other's hands. Catt watched the mother's face. She seemed to be fighting back tears. The father's lips were trembling.

A horrible thought occurred to Catt. Was Lemmy going to throw the baby into the water? It would make no sense at all, but still Catt's stomach knotted at the thought.

The plank was there though. Obviously, someone was going to walk across it. Sure enough, Lemmy clutched the crying baby close to his chest, and set one foot on the plank.

"We dedicate this new life to you, Tamathe, mother of the river," said Lemmy, walking slowly and steadily forward.

The plank bounced slightly. Catt edged closer to the trench, balancing on the bricks, wondering if she would need to jump in to save them.

"We name this child Nikeif, hear it now, Mother Tamathe, carry the sound of her name in your waters, all the way to the sea, and bless this child all the way through her life," said Lemmy.

Catt was absolutely certain that not a single drop of water from this irrigation ditch would ever reach the sea. There was so much desert, she wasn't even sure which way the closest sea might be.

Lemmy reached the other side and stepped off the plank. He delivered little Nikeif, still crying, into her parents' waiting arms. The two of them sank to their knees, cradling the infant between them, kissing each other, kissing the baby's forehead, and weeping in what Catt guessed was probably joy.

Catt waited for Lemmy's signal, and then set about retrieving the plank. She quickly found that lifting it up from this position was considerably more difficult than laying it down had been, and she very nearly dropped it into the trench. She was aware that this simple plank was probably quite valuable. There were exceedingly few trees in the city, so it was likely that most lumber came in with the caravans.

Back on the road, the parents thanked High Priest Lemmy profusely. They strapped the now-calm Nikeif back into her sling on her father's back. The mother clasped Lemmy's hands and spoke earnestly to him for a while. Catt waited with the plank over her shoulder.

The woman then came over to Catt and took her free hand and pressed a few coins into it. "Thank you much strong woman," she said in a thick accent. "You bear bridge well. My God honor."

# Districts

Later, after they had parted ways with the grateful parents and returned to the Polypantheonic Temple, Catt asked Lemmy, "How much are these coins actually worth?"

She had leaned the plank up against the wall in the back of the Temple, and was now counting the coins. There were the three silver ones the judge had given her, and now she had seven of the small copper coins.

Lemmy gave Catt another silver coin. "These are Shmouds," he said. "The smaller ones are Thorbs. Twenty Thorbs adds up to one Shmoud. I can pay you one Shmoud each day for helping me. I fear it is no kind of a fortune, but it will be enough for food and lodging in the Poor Quarter."

"The Poor Quarter?" Catt asked, wrinkling her nose. She sat down on the front pew so she could speak to Lemmy without looming over him.

"That would be the part of the city in that direction." Lemmy waved both hands generally away from the mountains, towards the direction of the desert.

"And they actually call it that?" asked Catt.

"I'm afraid so. It's always been called that, as far as I know."

"And what is this part of the city called?" Catt inquired.

"We are currently in the district called *Marketday*," said Lemmy, "And up against the mountains is *Old Bakak*." Lemmy pointed in the direction of the palace.

"What was the place we walked to today?"

"That was *Granary Hill*," said Lemmy, "and in the opposite direction is *Temple Hill*, where the university is... I do suppose that one is confusingly named, as most of the temples are in Old Bakak."

"It's still a better name than Poor Quarter." Catt pointed out.

Lemmy laughed, "Fair. Perhaps you should petition the King to rename it?"

At the mention of the King, Catt suddenly thought of Segna's beautiful face, and soft hands, and of her shapely collarbones and neck...

Neck.

Catt's stomach turned, and she wanted to think about something else instead.

"Anyways," said Catt. "What is next? You have more appointments today?"

"I do," confirmed Lemmy. "Just a few blessings, and a support group meeting. But I shall be able to handle it all myself. I think you should go and find some lodging, and rest, and seek some peace of mind. I feel guilty already for having put you to work on the same day you were freed from prison."

"That's okay," Catt said, "It was good to have something to do. The baby was cute, and I think my legs needed the walk."

"Very well then, we shall start fresh tomorrow morning. Go now, find yourself a place to stay."

"Any advice on how exactly?" asked Catt, standing.

"Skip the Inns, I dare say," suggested Lemmy. "Plenty of the apartment houses will have rooms available, if you just ask around, you should be able to find something for two or three Shmouds a week, I imagine."

Catt nodded, doing simple math in her head. She stood up. "Thank you Lemmy. I think I will manage. I am looking forward to more acolyting."

"May all the gods bless you, my friend," said Lemmy.

Catt waved, and walked out of the Polypantheonic Temple. It was true, she thought, that she actually was looking forward to doing odd jobs for the eccentric priest. It was simple honest work, but she had a feeling it wouldn't be dull. She also likes the idea of having safe legal employment in a place where the law seemed especially harsh. It would give her time and opportunity to become more comfortable with her surroundings before she risked any more lucrative schemes.

# Advisors

As a professor, Segna Ur-Segna knew that very little in the way of academics would get done in the first week of a new semester. It was an orientation week. The first week was a time to make sure the students understood the scope of the class, and the difficulty and dangers of the magic they would be learning. It was a time for lesson plans and outlines, and assessments, and rushing off to buy that book or reagent that had been on the syllabus when one enrolled in the class, but that one had forgotten to bring to class.

That was what Segna's first week as King had felt like; A kingship orientation week. There had been introductions to various hereditary nobles, to the masters of the trade guilds, to the consuls and diplomats of assorted foreign city-states. There had been the tours of the different wings of her vast palace. There had been her many advisors, each explaining what topics they would specialize in advising her about. There had been clothiers measuring and consulting on the style of the royal wardrobe, and artists and builders proposing personalizations of her living quarters.

Segna had been excited about all this for the first few days, but now she was growing impatient. She wanted to actually wield her power on something more important than the cut of her own dress or the art on the walls of her bedroom.

She was pleased then, when a group of advisors approached her after breakfast, and announced that it was time to review incomplete projects from her predecessor, and decide which ones to complete.

"It is traditional," disclosed the Visor of Protocol, "to sustain all such decrees, out of respect for one's antecessor."

"Of course." Segna agreed. She understood the default of respect for the old king, and she imagined that she would want her own policies to continue beyond her death.

"All except for the most ill-advised ones," contradicted the Chief Admonisher, with a sour frown on their face.

"It is a mere formality we must observe," insisted the Visor of Protocol, with an angry glance at the Chief Admonisher.

"And an important safeguard," countered the Admonisher.

The Steward of Precedent chimed in, "Indeed it is so! Just five years ago, the incoming King exercised their authority to decline to implement several of their predecessor's debt cancellations."

"How about we just get started?" suggested King Segna.

The Prime Archivist began to read off a list of unimplemented decrees from the last few weeks of the old king's reign. Many of them were small adjustments in the tax rates of various import and export commodities.

Segna approved of each of them with the formal words, "Sustained by my own decree."

"His ex-majesty was deeply interested in the health of the economy," the Treasurer-in-Politic apologetically explained.

"More like he was manipulating the futures markets!" interjected the Chief Admonisher.

The Treasurer made an indignant noise, and the Prime Archivist growled at them both, offended at being interrupted.

"I'll just sustain them all for now," said Segna. "I can review tax policy later."

"You need to say the words for *each*!" whined the Visor of Protocol. "It's tradition."

"What if I decree that I don't have to say the words for each?" asked Segna, more as a joke than as a serious inquiry.

The Visor of Protocol looked as if they had been slapped.

"You can, of course, make any royal decree you wish your majesty," said a high pitched voice. It was the Seneschal of Delays. "But seeing as alterations to the forms and protocols of governance can have profound impact on the Rule of Law, any such decrees have an automatic 10 week implementation delay, and must be reviewed by the High Court."

"Fine, fine. Sustained by my own decree," relented Segna.

The Visor of Protocol and the Prime Archivist both looked enormously relieved. The Chief Admonisher chuckled.

The Archivist continued with the list, and Segna continued sustaining the decrees. She remembered that the mandatory delays on many of her decrees had been explained to her a few days ago, but there had been so much that she had failed to absorb it all. She knew it was the job of the Seneschal of Delays to keep track of these rules so that she did not need to memorize them herself, but she had the feeling that learning how exactly the delays limited her power was going to be important if she expected to be an effective King.

# Alone

That afternoon, after an interminable luncheon with representatives of the Farmer's Guild and the Quarrymaster's Guild, each of whom were advocating subtly different amendments to a proposed royal decree regarding new aqueduct construction, King Segna decided she needed some time to herself.

The Visor of Protocol and the Chief Admonisher were hovering about, even when she returned to her personal quarters, so she drove them away by declaring that she wished to make use of the royal bathing pool.

"Very well," sniffed the Visor. "It is an important part of the royal prerogative."

"It's good to be King," said the Admonisher, with apparent jealousy, and they both took their leave of her.

Then Segna had to convince the pool attendants that she did not need any help, and that she could safely operate the bath all on her own. This proved even more difficult than ridding herself of the advisors, and finally she had to order them, by royal decree, to take the afternoon off with pay and go home and leave her alone. At least there were *some* types of decrees she could make without an implementation delay.

This was effective, but the attendants insisted on bringing an advisor back to witness the decree, so they would not be accused of abandoning their posts.

The Visor of Protocol arched an eyebrow curiously at all this, but after the attendants were sent away, the Visor promised to set a guard on the outer door to ensure that Her Majesty would not be disturbed in any way.

Finally alone, Segna operated the pump handle that allowed her to fill her own bath. The royal bathing pool was not large. It did not take long to fill the concavity in the center of the beautiful tile floor of the royal bath house.

Segna disrobed, and placed her feet in the water. She was a little surprised at how cold it was.

In the midst of the perennial drought of Great Bakak, city wedged between desert and arid mountains, a real bathtub was an extreme luxury. Under normal circumstances, *"bathing"* meant sand-scrubs, perfumed oils, and wet spongecloth. A half-filled bucket of water was sufficient for good hygiene, and it was all that Segna was accustomed to.

She had been shown the royal bathing pool on her first day as King, but this was the first time she had actually used it. Segna carefully lowered herself into the water, shivering a little. She sank until her breasts were submerged under the surface. She found that the sloped side of the pool was angled just right so she could rest the back of her head and neck against it, and although the tiles were hard, it was comfortable.

Segna stretched out her feet until they touched the opposite side of the pool, but that left the tops of her knees still protruding from the water a bit, and not until she twisted them sideways a little did they vanish beneath the water.

It felt utterly alien to be submerged in water like this. It was somehow even more unnatural than the prickling heavy feeling of working a magic spell.

Segna looked at the way the surface of the water moved. She realized that the varying blue shades of the tile work covering the rest of the bath house's floor must be meant to invoke the impression that the pool was much larger than it was, and she pondered the idea of so much water. She swished her arms back and forth experimentally, and made small tentative splashes. She felt a little bit guilty, which she knew was irrational, because, as the pool attendants had explained to her before, the water would not be wasted. When she was finished it would drain away and join the reserves of water destined to irrigate the farming terraces in Granary Hill.

Segna splashed some water into her face, and onto her shaved head. The idea of ducking her head under the water entirely wandered through her imagination, but it was too frightening. The idea set her to shivering again, and she nearly jumped up out of the water, but by planting her hands on the solid tiles and breathing deeply, she was able to calm herself down.

Segna's shoulders shook, and it was not entirely from the cold.

There had been so much change in her life so suddenly. She missed her classroom. She missed her old flat in Temple Hill. She couldn't go back there, it wasn't hers anymore. Royal servants had gone there and collected her things, and they were now stacked in boxes along the wall of a storage room in the palace. Someone else was probably living there now.

Someone else would be teaching her classes too. She wondered who. It occurred to Segna that she could make a royal decree, and they would have to let her return to the University– perhaps after a delay– and let her continue teaching Arcane Geometry for Intermediate Wizards, but she could guess what sort of chaos that might cause. To say the least, it would disrupt the learning environment. It would be selfish. She couldn't stop being King. Being King gave her the power to impose her will, but imposing her will wasn't what she wanted.

Segna splashed some more water on her face as if to wash away tears. She didn't want to feel sorry for herself. She didn't want to waste her time and energy wishing that things had happened differently. Not even the most powerful magic could change the past.

Segna tried to think about what she actually *did* want. She floated motionless in the water. She watched the ripples gradually diminish.

"I want to be a good King," Segna said out loud. "I want to make the best use of what fate has handed to me."

That seemed right, but knowing it and saying it were one thing, and actually figuring out how to accomplish it was quite another.

As the water grew more still, Segna looked at herself. She saw the letters of the spell tattooed on her body. She was proud of that spell. It had been hard work to compose it. The letters were upside-down and distorted by the water, but she knew them all by heart.

Segna's lips moved, and in a whisper, she recited the words of the spell, substituting the appropriate variables, and computing the correct whole. She felt the draw of magic, the stretching of space, the tingle of brief un-reality.

For a long dark breathless shapeless moment, Segna felt herself in that void nowhere-ness that was not part of the real world. Then she snapped back into reality, standing now, square in the bath house door with not a single drop of water on her. Her spell had teleported her, and left the water behind. She watched the surprisingly violent splash as the water crashed into the body-shaped pocket of vacuum she had left in the pool when she teleported away.

Yes, she was proud of that spell. She took a robe from a hook on the wall and put it on. It was her own spell, created from first principles. It was unique, and totally unlike the textbook teleportation spells that other wizards used, with their painstaking and time-consuming synchronization of magic circles. Segna's spell only worked over extremely short distances, and she couldn't take anything with her, which made it a commercially unworkable spell, but it was hers, and it was special.

Segna operated the lever that allowed the pool's water to drain away in a little vortex.

Surely somehow she could learn enough about how to wield her royal power to create something from it that was *hers* and something that was *special*. A single year was not a lot of time, but it had to be possible. If she could master magic, she could master kingship.

# Bucket

Catt carried the empty bucket down the stairs, four flights. On the ground floor, Catt saw that the Landlady's door was open. Light spilled out from a small candle. This apartment building was far enough from the city's center that it was outside the range of the mysterious Unburning curse, so fire was possible here. Fire was also illegal here, but apparently that particular law was not enforced very strictly.

Catt could see the old woman asleep in a rocking chair. Her wrinkled hands were folded around a half closed book. She had antlers on top of her head, sprouting from her wispy white hair like a velvety pair of mirrored trees.

Catt wondered why the Landlady slept with the door open. She had been renting a room in this building for several days now, and every night she had seen the door ajar.

Catt proceeded past the Landlady's door to the front door. This one, at least, was closed. Catt opened it carefully, trying to minimize the squeak of the hinges. She went down the two stone steps to the street, and tarried to look at the moon. It was waxing in the night sky, and she could see it in the gap between the two tenement buildings across the street.

A handful of people were out on the street, and at a glance it was not easy to tell which ones might be up to no good under cover of night, and which ones were just neighbors taking advantage of the pleasant coolness of the nocturnal dark.

Catt circled around the side of the building to the water pump that was shared by her own building and three others.

The Landlady had explained, "Yon pump works better at night, dearie." And Catt had learned that this was true.

Catt placed her bucket under the spout and began to work the handle. In a moment a trickle of rusty water spurt forth. During the day, the most that would emanate from the pump were gurgling noises.

By the time the bucket was full, Catt's arm was aching pleasantly, and she could feel her heart beating faster. She hefted the bucket, and carried it back around, inside, and up the stairs, taking care not to spill any.

Catt's room was on the fifth floor. It was small and irregularly shaped, but Catt liked it. For the moment at least, it was home.

She took the bucket to the small countertop by the window where the moonlight streamed in. She let it settle for a moment, and then used a big tin ladle to scoop water into three bottles. Into each she added a single drop of a purple tincture. Then she corked each bottle, shook each vigorously, and lined them up by the window. By midnight they would be drinkable– if a bit odd-tasting. The small apartment had already been equipped with these accoutrements of water purification when Catt moved in, and she was growing accustomed to the ritual of using them each night.

She put two more drops of tincture in the bucket and stirred it up. She had been told that this was not essential if the water was just to be used for washing up, but that it was common to do it anyway "for good luck," as the Landlady had put it.

Catt fetched a red fruit from her pack, and ate it while staring thoughtfully at the moon. The fruit resembled a plum in every way except for its spicy aftertaste. She wasn't sure what it was called. A substantial amount of stringy pulp clung to the pit of the fruit. Catt leaned forward, stretching on her toes, and set the pit down on the brick ledge just outside the windowsill. Catt had been reading about Hret-ret-akl in the book Lemmy had leant to her. There were a few other fruit pits already on the ledge, in various states of decay and desiccation. They were not actually devotional offerings to the goddess of rotting food, rather, Catt thought of them as experiments. They were a sort of a probe to test whether or not the goddess was watching. Catt thought it far-fetched that a forest goddess would pay any attention to what was happening in a distant desert, but Lemmy seemed to believe that gods could hear their followers regardless of distance, so Catt was at least willing to entertain the idea. She had noticed that although the remains of the fruit outside her open window had attracted the attention of ants and gnats, she had not been bothered by the creatures inside the apartment. Catt wasn't ready to interpret this as a divine sign, but she did take note of it.

Catt dunked a clean rag into the water bucket and washed her face and hands. A proper sponge bath could wait for morning. She stripped down to her undergarments and retired to the narrow bed tucked in the back of the apartment.

Sleep would come easily.

Or so Catt imagined. She had worked hard all day, and her muscles felt tired. It was surprising how much lifting and carrying was involved in setting up and tearing down the essentials and decorations of a dozen different religious ceremonies in the same day. Catt was able to transform the main room of the Polypantheonic Temple into whatever shrine or sanctuary it needed to become, and she could do it in a fraction of the time it used to take Lemmy. In the time since Catt had become an acolyte, Lemmy had been able to almost double the number of worshipers he could book for appointments.

But Catt hadn't just been lifting and shifting heavy holy items. Sometimes Lemmy would shove an open book into her hand and say, "This passage, if you please." Then she would be reading a prayer or a blessing in a solemn voice while he lit candles, or beat a drum, or smeared honey-mud on worshiper's foreheads.

In moments like that, Catt felt like a fraud, as if she was betraying these people by pretending to be a holy person and speaking words that meant so much to them while the importance of the words flowing out of her mouth was a complete mystery to herself.

Then when the service or ceremony was over, these people would seem happy, or emotional, or uplifted, and they would look at her with eyes full of respect, and thank her with just as much respect as they would give to the High Priest. People were allowing her to be a part of their spiritual hopes and fears and accepting her as a part of their veneration of their gods.

This odd mixture of feeling inadequate and feeling embraced all at once was both unsettling and thrilling. If this job had been a con, and she had been helping Lemmy fleece unsuspecting prey, she would have been on more comfortable and familiar ground, but she would have also grown bored after a while and moved on to look for some other racket.

The Polypantheonic Temple was no racket. It was completely sincere, in all its muddled and improvised theology. Certainly Lemmy was collecting donations, sometimes generous ones, sometimes pittances, sometimes nothing at all, but there was no wealth. Wherever the wealthy and privileged of the city worshiped, it wasn't at the Polypantheonic Temple. It was a place for poor immigrants and lonely outcasts, and small close-knit families and tribes who clung to strange faiths from far away places.

Something about this honest– if peculiar– work had grabbed at Catt's soul, and made her heart ache in a way that made her look forward to tomorrow with excitement, while simultaneously perturbing her sleep, and leaving her tossing and turning on her narrow bed in her rented room in this exotic unfamiliar city which was already inexorably beginning to feel like home.

## Measure

Senior Executioner Crocken walked briskly along Sausage Row in the pre-dawn light.

Sausage Row was the major street that cut in a straight line through the Poor Quarter, connecting Marketday to the Smokefields. Even though it was early, there was already plenty of traffic, animal-drawn carts in the road, porters with baskets, vendors pushing wheeled carts. Sausage Row was the artery by which hot breakfast made its way from the kitchens of the Smokefields to the hungry soon-to-be-waking citizens of the rest of Great Bakak.

Crocken wasn't interested in breakfast. He had already eaten a good healthy meal, cold, cheap, and nourishing. Crocken was here to take the Measurement.

He reached a place in the street that didn't look particularly different than any other, unless one was aware of its significance. He walked to the side of the street.

Crocken looked at the flagstones around his feet. There were many chalk marks here, in parallel lines. He fished the tools of the Measurement out of the inner pocket of his voluminous black cape. A large candle, a flint striker, and a piece of chalk.

He crouched on the side of the road, dropped the chalk, and expertly positioned the wick of the candle into the striker. With a few dozen quick motions of his right hand he managed to get the wick to ignite. He let it burn for a moment to make sure it wouldn't sputter out, and then he dropped the flint striker back into the pocket and picked up the chalk.

After just a moment to savor the scent of hot tallow as it wafted past his mask, Crocken began the ritual of sliding the candle low over the flagstones, parallel to the direction of the street.

As Crocken slowly moved the candle, the flame abruptly winked out of existence without even a curl of smoke.

Crocken made a small chalk mark directly beneath the candle. Then he fetched the striker back out of his pocket, skillfully re-lit the candle, and repeated the whole performance.

When the flame again vanished in exactly the same place, he overlaid the small chalk mark with a big decisive chalk line.

Crocken pinched and twisted the charred wick. He dropped it and the chalk into his pocket, and took out the final tool of the Measurement, a short length of yarn. He used it to measure the distance between the new chalk line, and the old chalk line that he had drawn a week previously. The distance was a bit more than the width of his hand. He tied a knot in the yarn to mark the distance, and this too went back in the pocket.

Crocken stood, and looked at the chalk marks that spread down the street towards the Smokefields. It never rained in Great Bakak, so the chalk was never completely washed away. The passage of many feet eventually scuffed it enough to obscure the lines, but there were still enough of the weekly marks visible to show a clear picture. The Unburning was shrinking, and it was shrinking faster as time went on. It wouldn't reach Marketday in his lifetime, but some day it would get there.

Crocken became aware that someone was looking at him. He turned his mask towards the person.

It was a sinewy woman carrying a large bundle over her shoulder. She had red hair, small horns, and curious eyes.

Her curious eyes immediately looked away. She shifted her burden to the other shoulder to make it look as if that was why she had been tarrying, and then walked away down the street with a forced purposefulness.

Crocken thought her suspicious, so he made an effort to memorize her features, and then let her go, and turned back the other way to deliver the Measurement back to the headquarters. The rate at which the Unburning was decaying was important public information and would be recorded in the guild ledgers.

# Not Food

Catt stared at the Executioner who was crouching on his hands and knees at the side of the street. He was doing something interesting with a piece of chalk and a bit of string. There were a lot of chalk marks on the stones, almost as if he was playing some sort of child's game.

Other people on the street hardly seemed to notice him, and Catt wondered at that too.

Suddenly he looked up, right at her. Catt's heart thumped, but she kept her cool and pretended to be adjusting the sacrifice she was carrying, and then nonchalantly continued on her way. What did she have to worry about anyway? She hadn't committed any crimes since getting out of prison, not even little ones! Her "intercessor" would vouch for that if she was questioned.

Catt was headed for the Smokefields this morning, and she was excited to see it first-hand for the first time. She knew its reputation by now, and had smelled it when the wind was favorable, and she anticipated a smoky wonderland of campfires and kitchen-pits. She had a job to do, of course, but that didn't change the fact that her mouth was watering and her stomach was rumbling.

The close, tall buildings gradually gave way to open spaces, and Sausage Row began to twist a bit as it started to rise uphill. The Smokefields appeared to be built atop a rocky irregular ridge separating the south edge of the city from the desert.

Catt noted the dramatic shift of architecture. Stone steps crisscrossed the craggy hills, and low stone walls were everywhere, some built with obvious purpose, but others in locations that made no sense at all. None of the walls were very tall, most of them not even coming up to Catt's belly-button. The walls, however, were insignificant beneath the tents. Everywhere were tents, some small, some colossal, all stained black by the smoke, only showing white canvas where they had been patched and repaired after a thousand tiny accidental fires. Catt had seen the largest of these from a distance and taken them for steeply sloped rooftops, only now that she walked among them was it obvious that they were tents.

The air was warm here and full of smoke and drifting embers, but what commanded Catt's attention most was the smell of the air. This place was the kitchen of the whole city. There were smells of many kinds. Unpleasant smells were present, the smoke itself, as well as abattoir smells, smells of decay, but those were pushed back and overwhelmed by the good smells, the wonderful delicious smells. The smell of cooking food was so powerful that Catt could hardly think straight.

Lemmy had given her directions, but Catt still felt a bit disoriented. She decided to ask for help.

She saw a man coming down some steps with a basket on his shoulders.

"Excuse me!" Catt accosted the stranger. "Do you know where to find the Outer Bakak Fine Meats Company?"

The man looked at her with an expression of indifference. He was wearing a white sleeveless shirt, and a white cap, and his ears and lower lip bristled with silver rings and studs.

"Up that way," he said, gesturing with his chin. "Almost to the top, on the right. They have a sign."

"Thanks!" said Catt, but she noticed that the man's face, which had started out uninterested, had morphed into a scowl of bitter suspicion as he spoke.

She started to move away in the direction he had indicated, but suddenly he was following her.

"What's that you're carrying?" the man demanded.

"Stuff. None of your business," Catt replied, instantly defensive in reaction to his tone. She kept moving.

The man kept pace with her. "You don't look like a Porter," he said accusingly. "Where's your cap? Where's your badge?" He momentarily took one hand off the basket, balancing it as he tapped something yellow and orange embroidered on his sleeveless white shirt.

"I'm not a Porter," said Catt. She cut diagonally across the path to put more distance between herself and the man.

"Then what's that you're carrying? There damn well better not be food in there! Nobody carries food in this city without a Porter's badge!" He was almost shouting now, and had followed Catt, still crowding her.

The man began trying to sniff the big bag on Catt's shoulder. He was so close that she could smell the roast carrots in his basket.

Catt whirled away from him, bringing up one arm as a defensive ruse, as she simultaneously lowered her center of gravity and then slammed into him with the full weight of her body, knocking the aggressive man completely off his feet.

He skidded several places down the hill, lid flying off his basket. A few carrots escaped into the air, but amazingly he managed to keep the basket upright as he landed, saving most of them.

The man cursed and scrambled upright. "Nobody carries food without a badge!" he hissed. "The guild will hear about this! I won't forget this!"

"This isn't food!" Catt said forcefully. "You wanna check? Come on, I dare you to come check." Catt beckoned tauntingly with one hand, while the other hand hovered at her side. Her sword was long gone, but she had a cheap-yet-serviceable knife strapped discreetly to her flank.

The man's eyes blazed with spite. "You've made an enemy today. I won't forget this," he threatened, but he kept his distance now, shifting sideways to retrieve his basket lid.

Then without another word, he was hastily retreating down the hill towards Sausage Row, leaving only muddy carrots in the wake of his wrath.

"Not food!" Catt shouted after him. She waited until he was out of sight and then continued up the hill.

# Offering

Catt's blood was still pounding in her ears from the altercation. She had reached the sign marking the kitchen complex of the Outer Bakak Fine Meats And Sausages Company. She stood for a moment to calm herself and to survey her surroundings. The complex was dominated by one colossal smoke-blackened tent as high as a three story building. Catt could see the skeletal shapes of inner support beams as the gentle breeze caught the tent's canvas like it was the sail of a battleship. She could see distortions from heat in the air above the towering peak of the tent.

The hand-painted sign next to the path made the identity of the tent obvious, but no door was in evidence, so Catt circled the tent looking for one.

There were several other smaller tents surrounding the larger one. Catt spotted a person emerging from one of them. It was a tall woman wearing a blood-splattered white smock. She had long grey hair pinned back by long wing-like ears, and her face was lined with age in a way that contrasted sharply to her ramrod straight posture. She was holding a rope tied to some small pigs who were walking single file in strange silence.

"Hi, you know where I could find–" Catt began, but as she spoke, the pigs all began squealing at once and pulling in different directions on the rope.

"Oh, now you've done it!" exclaimed the woman, exasperated. "You've broken the spell. I'll have to start over!" She dragged the squealing pigs back into the smaller tent, muttering irritably.

"Sorry?" Catt offered, but the woman was already gone.

Catt looked in the direction that the woman had first been heading, and she spotted an open flap in the back of the big tent.

As she approached the flap, Catt could feel the air moving. Outside air was being drawn powerfully into the flap.

Catt stepped inside and looked around, then immediately looked up. Her eye was drawn by a powerful red glow emanating from above.

A giant fire was burning in the middle of an elevated platform halfway up the tent. There were ladders and catwalks criss-crossing the space between her and the bonfire. She could feel the radiant heat of the fire, but she could also feel the flow of air being pulled in and up as if the whole tent was an immense chimney.

The ground floor of the tent was occupied by various workstations, racks of butcher knives, coils of sausage casings, shelves of rock salt and spice jars, and huge long-handled grinders. The appearance of the place was visually overwhelming, and more than just a little bit frightening.

A big person was sitting astride a nearby grinding wheel. Sparks were flying from the edge of a cleaver as the wheel spun. The person seemed to notice Catt. They stopped working the pedal and set the cleaver down on a nearby table.

"Hullo!"

"Hi!" said Catt. She had to raise her voice. "I'm looking for someone named Provincial!" Even with the noise of the grinding wheel fading away, the roar of the fire and the rushing wind made it hard to be heard.

"That's me!" shouted the big person. He was not tall, but he was quite wide. His mouth was a broad friendly grin under a bulbous nose. His eyes were tiny and black, and bushy eyebrows like umbrellas protected them from the beads of sweat on his shiny bald head. While his crown was gleamingly hairless, his moustache and sideburns compensated by merging together into curly golden locks almost the width of his shoulders.

"You must be the Reverend Lemmy's acolyte! Most pleased to meet you," shouted Provincial. "This is the burnt offerings?" he asked, indicating Catt's bag.

"Yes!" said Catt. "Can we talk outside? It's loud in here!"

They exited the tent, and were able to exchange pleasantries without shouting.

"It is a big bag! I'll fetch a large rack," said Provincial, after Catt had introduced herself and shaken his hand.

"Business is booming," Catt affirmed.

Provincial brought a large mesh tray, and Catt opened up the bag of sacrifices. Together they began unpacking objects and placing them on the tray. There were all sorts of things; wooden idols, bundles of dry leaves, crude cloth dolls, folded articles of clothing, clay crafts, hand-written scrolls, and even a few small cakes.

Catt thought of the man who had accosted her and accused her of carrying food. She was glad she had not known the cakes were there.

Catt noticed that the sleeveless white shirt that Provincial wore had the same yellow-and-orange embroidered badge that she had seen on the hostile man's shirt. It looked something like a stylized candle flame.

"What's that symbol you are wearing?" Catt asked. Provincial had been nothing but pleasant so far, but she still felt cautious about asking.

"Why this? This, it is the badge of the Cook's Guild," Provincial said, pointing to his chest with obvious pride.

"On my way here, someone with the same badge harassed me. I had to knock him down."

"Oh, my! Do tell!" Provincial exclaimed sympathetically.

After Catt had told him the whole story, Provincial frowned and snorted. "I think I have seen the man of which you speak. Damn his face! These Porters, they can be very territorial, and is true, you must have a Porter's card to carry food for commercial purposes, but this one, I think, he is overstepping. It is good that you knock him down!" He laughed a little at this last.

"I just don't want to tangle with him again," said Catt. "I don't want to get in trouble with the guild or the law for any further damage I might do to him."

Provincial chuckled. "I will mention his bad conduct to the guild chiefs, and if I see him myself I put a little warning in him, yes?"

Catt smiled, "Thanks, Provincial."

They had finished arranging the sacrifices on the rack. Each of them had small slips of paper tied to them, each naming a worshiper and a deity in Lemmy's careful handwriting. These flapped in the breeze as Catt and Provincial carried the rack back inside the tent.

Provincial directed them to some stairs that led up to a platform closer to the fire. They placed the rack of offerings down on the end of the platform.

From this close, the intensity of the fire heated Catt's face. It wasn't enough to be painful, but it was uncomfortable, and it made her perspire.

The big fire was strangely beautiful. It was held in a sort of bowl-shaped brazier, and she could see how it was fed with fuel from the side. Up above the flame, and all around it was a fantastical snarl of thick wires. The wires traced about like cobwebs and formed supports for trays of sliced meats, scaffolding for coils of plump sizzling sausages, and supported hooks which in turn supported whole slabs of roasting meat. Some parts of the wire glowed dully red from protracted contact with the fire.

"Put the sacrifices up high, above the fire!" Provincial shouted.

Catt stared at him in open-mouthed bewilderment, not understanding how he expected her to even begin doing such a task.

Four hook-tipped wires suddenly dipped down from above and fastened themselves to the corners of the burnt offering rack. They began to lift it up by some unseen mechanism.

Catt whistled in surprise, and stepped back a bit. She wiped the sweat off her forehead and looked up, watching the rack rise.

"How did you do that, magic?" Catt asked.

Provincial was still focusing his attention upwards. "Good, good!" He shouted. "Perhaps move those ribs to the side for now, we do not want them full of the wrong kind of smoke!"

A large rack of ribs moved laterally. Catt felt certain that this was some kind of spell, but Provincial's words did not sound anything like the utterings of a wizard, which she knew had to be spoken in specific special languages in order to work.

Provincial nodded in approval of the current position of the tray. The paper and cloth bits were already kindling. He seemed to belatedly notice Catt's curious amazement.

"Ha! You like? Is not magic," Provincial chuckled, "Is Jangley!"

"Jangley?" Catt asked, confused.

"Well, Jangley is maybe sort of magic. Jangley! Come down and meet Catt!"

All the wires lurched just slightly all at once, and then the cobweb began to rearrange itself, bunching downward. The rack of burnt offerings and the various cooking meats all remained in roughly the same places, with wires shifting and trading places to keep them where they were.

At the heart of the mass of wire, it seemed like there was one point where many of them came together in a bundle. This point was coming closer to Catt. She could see a cylindrical shape about as big as three fists side-by-side. The wires connected to its two ends as if it was their source. As it drew parallel to them, she could see a semi-round shape on the side of it that looked like a large eye.

"What is it?" Catt asked. It brought to mind a spider with far too many spindly legs, or some baleful ocean creature, all tentacles.

"Catt, meet Jangley. Jangley is a wire golem. Jangley, meet Catt Zago. She is the acolyte for Reverend Lemmy."

The wire golem was frightening, but Catt remained calm. It helped that Provincial was speaking to it like a person, but she was also glad that it was moving slowly.

"Pleased to make your acquaintance, Jangley," Catt said. She kept her hand firmly at her side. She did not want to shake any of its appendages, some of which were still glowing red hot.

"I like Small Priest," said a buzzing voice like a bucket full of bees. "If Small Priest apprentice you then I like you."

"Jangley is our Master Chef," said Provincial. "Jangley is the one whom we have to thank for the success of the Outer Bakak Fine Meats and Sausages Company. There is no finer chef in the Smokefields."

"I like to cook. I cannot taste," said Jangley's buzzing voice. "Will you taste for me?"

A thick slice of bacon descended from above on a single wire. It was sizzling and sputtering. Catt remembered how hungry she was, but she didn't dare burn her fingers by reaching for it. She also could not help but notice the wire's resemblance to a fishing line.

"Um... I..." Catt stalled, not wanting to offend the golem.

Provincial produced a grease-stained cloth pot holder from somewhere and held it under the bacon, as if he had seen this sort of interaction before and understood the need to put her at ease. Jangley gingerly dropped the bacon onto the cloth, and Provincial passed it to Catt. She blew on it to cool it and gratefully savored the smell.

After it had cooled enough that Catt could take a bite, Jangley asked, "Taste?"

"It is exquisite!" said Catt, honestly. She didn't know how to describe the smokey aftertaste, but she tried, "It tastes... like a beautiful flowering tree... burned to... the smoke... I'm sorry, that came out much more sad than I meant it to sound."

"It is good that sadness is in the taste," buzzed Jangley. "All meat has sadness, but you had empathy for the wood. This pleases me."

Catt nodded, unsure of how to respond. She ate the rest of the piece of bacon, chewing very slowly, feeling suddenly as if she had to relish the experience of eating it in order to respect the sorrow inherent in the meat.

"The offerings, they are burning well," said Provincial, changing the subject.

Catt looked up. Jangley also rotated the cylinder that seemed to be its head. The eye had a look about it that was very much like a person's eye.

The tray of sacrifices was now completely engulfed in flames.

"I hope the gods can taste the smoke," said Jangley. It turned its eye back towards Catt. "You are apprentice priest. Can you speak a prayer for me?"

Catt had no idea how to say a prayer, but she found herself asking, "To what god?"

Jangley's head swung side to side. "Not to sun goddess, not to sun god. I like the sun. I want a prayer just to the sun, not to any other."

"I'm still learning. I don't know how to pray that," Catt admitted. "But when I learn how, I would be happy to come back and pray for you."

Some of Jangley's wires rippled. "I would like this. I am patient," they buzzed. Then Jangley's eye turned away and the cylinder slowly pulled itself upward towards the fire, rearranging the web of wires as it went. The conversation was over.

Outside the tent Catt said goodbye to Provincial.

"They never asked Reverend Lemmy to pray for them before, I did not expect it," Provincial told her. "Jangley must like you very much I think."

Catt thought about this as she walked back towards the Polypantheonic Temple. She felt the morning sun shining on her, and wondered how to make the prayer that Jangley had asked for.

# Rain

Catt lay sprawled on a wooden pew in the Polypantheonic Temple. She was resting after a busy day of blessings, religious sing-alongs, and one funeral for an old man who had, in life, worshiped the twin beer-brewing gods of the distant Odok Barrens.

Catt was not drunk, but she was light-headed. It had been a really good funeral.

Catt was not just resting, and she was not just waiting for her head to clear. She was also reading– studying. A few weeks ago, when she had returned from meeting Jangley, she had asked Lemmy to teach her how to compose new prayers.

Reading prayers was easy, and memorizing and reciting them was not much harder. Catt was good at memorizing things when she put her mind to it, and prayers tended to be a cinch since they so often had a lot of rhythm and repetition to them.

Lemmy had advised her that the invention of new prayers was a combination of intuiting what the worshiper needed to hear, and understanding what the deity wanted to hear. Catt had not yet figured out how to apply this to Jangley's request, but she had been reading books of collected prayers for ideas. She was especially confounded by the stipulation that it be a prayer to the sun itself. Catt didn't know much about the sun other than it lived in the sky and was too bright to look at. Lemmy had suggested that she read about various sun goddesses and gods from different lands in order to learn about the sun.

It was this that she was currently doing. There seemed to be a lot of business about invisible things in the sky, chariots that carried the sun, serpents that devoured it, ladders that it climbed, benevolent giants that threw and caught the sun's sphere. She wasn't sure how useful all that was. When she blocked the sun's blinding radiance with her fingers and surveyed the sky immediately around it, she never saw anything else up there.

Lemmy was puttering around the temple, tidying up with a little broom. After a while, he settled by the door, and seemed to be staring at something outside. Catt ignored him and kept reading. She only had a few more minutes of good reading light before the sun went down, and she wasn't getting any closer to a satisfactory or consistent explanation of why the sun even did things like "go down".

"I do believe," said Lemmy, "that we are about to get some rain."

It was a mundane thing to say, but there was something in the way that Lemmy said it that got Catt's attention. He was speaking in a tone of awe and wonder that exceeded the level of reverence he usually showed to actual gods.

Catt placed a bookmark, dropped her divine encyclopedia, and got up to go and see what Lemmy was talking about.

The High Priest was standing on the cobbles outside the temple door, and craning his head up to the darkening sky. The sunset was a lot more colorful than it usually was, and there actually was a sparse blanket of clouds above.

As they stood there, a few drops of moisture began to fall.

"Praise every god!" Lemmy murmured.

As the rain fell, people stopped in the streets and spread their hands. People leaned out of upstairs windows, exclaiming and calling for their families to come and see. A coach that was rumbling down the street stopped, and the well-dressed passengers got out and stood around, catching the raindrops with their skyward faces. A group of children of various ages came tearing out from somewhere, laughing and screaming "Rain! Rain! Rain!" As they ran down the street.

The whole thing only lasted for about two minutes before the rain drops stopped falling, and the grey of the dissipating clouds gave way to the blue-black of twilight.

It had never fallen that hard. It hadn't even been enough to turn the dust in the street into mud, just enough to speckle it with tiny muddy ringlets. The moisture already seemed to be evaporating away.

Catt had been completely unimpressed by the rain, but she had found people's reaction to it quite delightful. Lemmy was now standing with a dreamy smile on his toothy face, and his hands clasped in front of him beatifically.

"It's been nearly sixty years since Great Bakak has been blessed by a rain storm!" Lemmy said. "I doubted whether I would get to see another in my lifetime!"

Catt was tickled by the idea of Lemmy describing what had just happened as a *storm*. "That was something alright," Catt said with a grin.

"Oh my!" Lemmy said suddenly, as if a realization had dawned on him. "I'll have to clear some room on the calendar tomorrow! We'll have to cancel some worship services!"

"Why?" asked Catt.

"We should expect an invitation from the Unchurch. They'll be throwing a party tomorrow."

"From the what?" Catt queried, not sure what an Unchurch was.

# Spectacle

As the most important honorary guest to the Rain Festival, King Segna Ur-Segna was the last to be seated. She entered the Grand Sanctuary of the Unchurch Against the Nameless Rain-god from a side-gallery, following behind her advisors.

The Unchurch had set up a gilded throne for her on the right side of the sanctuary. She mounted the three steps, raised her chin towards the Anti-bishop, as protocol dictated, and seated herself. She smoothed her shimmering blue gown over her knees, and tugging at a shoulder strap as inconspicuously as she could manage with a few thousand pairs of eyes trained on her. The neckline plunged a bit lower than she would have preferred, but her royal clothiers had spent all night in a sleepless frenzy making it especially for the occasion, and there had been no time for last-minute alterations.

The Anti-bishop made eye contact with her from his place behind the elevated podium, and then he turned to the congregation, and began to lead them in a song.

*"The Rain God Is Eternal—"*
*"The Rain God Hates Us All—"*
*"The Rain God Never Forgets Us—"*
*"The Rain God Never Forgives Us—"*

Segna surveyed the singing congregation. They filled the whole center of the Grand Sanctuary, seated in long rows and clad in various shades of blue. Guests of honor such as herself were arrayed on either side of the sanctuary, flanking the main congregation.

Segna spotted a group of judges from the high court dressed in robes and white wigs, but most of the other honored guests seemed to be priests from the other major temples of Great Bakak. Segna could see a delegation from the Healers of Essentyn to her left, and a group of high priests of the Reformed Seekers of Rest seated on the right.

*"...The Rain God, He Is The Worst—"*

***"For No Reason We Were Cursed—"***

Segna had not actually witnessed last night's rain. She had been in a meeting with the Treasurer-in-Politic, when a breathless servant had interrupted to tell her about it. By the time she had made it to a window, it was all over.

The Steward of Precedent had extolled the honor of having such an event occurred during her reign, and the Visor of Protocol had expounded the importance of the occasion to the Unchurch Against the Nameless Rain-god, which was numbered among the most important religions in Great Bakak.

***"...May His Name Forever Be—"***

***"Forgotten And Blasphemed By Hearts And Lips—"***

***"Forgotten And Blasphemed By Hearts... And... Liiiiiips."***

The last verse of the song was finished, and the last notes from the pipe organ lingered in the air.

The Anti-bishop spoke now, using some simple magic to amplify his voice so it boomed thunderously through the huge sanctuary.

"My Family! Honored guests! We are gathered here not to celebrate the rain which fell upon our parched land upon the yesterday, rather were are here to decry the miserly spite of that Nameless Rain-god who allows only such few paltry drops fall upon our proud city!"

"MAY HIS NAMELESS NAME BE DISHONORED!" chanted the whole congregation in unison.

Segna studied the crowd. They all held slips of paper, and each time the Anti-bishop would pause in his sermon, they would recite a verse to punctuate his words.

The Anti-bishop continued, "Through a thousand years of relentless drought, our ancestors learned that worship was pointless! All offerings were rejected, all sacrifices ignored! We gave our blood, we gave our tears, and our answer was only silence and desiccation."

"OUR BLOOD, OUR TEARS, ALL FOR NOTHING," chanted the crowd.

Segna stopped paying attention to the words, and for a while just listened to way they sounded, the amplified sonorous lilt of the Anti-bishop, and the mighty refrain of the congregation's reply.

The sermon went on for a long while, but finally the Anti-bishop seemed to be wrapping things up.

"I shall now partake in the Dry Sacrament!" declared the Anti-bishop.

Two acolytes approached him, one carried a small glass, and the other carried a small pitcher.

The Anti-bishop took the pitcher, and with fastidious care, allowed just two tiny drops to fall into the glass.

"These droplets represent the two meagre minutes of rain that were apportioned to us last night."

Another acolyte approached carrying a large tray of biscuits.

"These biscuits represent the long years of drought that we have been cursed with!"

The Anti-bishop began stuffing the biscuits into his mouth one after another. The dry crunching was audible throughout the sanctuary, magnified by the same magic that had been amplifying his voice. After the tray was emptied, and the Anti-bishop's cheeks were bulging with biscuits like he was some kind of nut-gathering rodent, he began to cough. Large crumbs fell from his mouth as he hacked and wheezed, chunks scattering and bouncing to the floor around him.

The acolyte proffered the glass, and the Anti-bishop took it quickly, though it was a moment before he could control the coughing enough to even attempt to throw his head back and drink from it.

It was impossible to tell whether the two drops of water made it into his mouth. He flung the empty glass to the floor where it shattered. Another acolyte appeared with a broom and cleaned it up.

As the Anti-bishop attempted to suppress the cough and swallow the remaining dry biscuit crumbs, a person on horseback entered the sanctuary from a side gallery.

"Now!" wheezed the Anti-bishop, finally regaining the use of his voice, "We shall collect an offering of alms for the poor!"

The white horse's hooves clicked on the marble floor.

A group of ushers carrying baskets moved through the sanctuary collecting coins.

Segna had known this part of the service was coming, and she had prepared for it. The Seneschal of Delays had assured her that for this special occasion, the Court would waive the usual implementation delay on the allocation of Royal funds for purposes of charity.

The Treasurer-in-Politic was carrying a very heavy bag of coins. After the ushers had completed their tour of the congregation, they brought the baskets before King Segna. She stood as the Treasurer poured the coins, topping off each basket in turn. There was a general murmur of approval from the room.

Finally, the baskets of coins were carried to the horse, and poured into its saddlebags.

The rider, who was dressed in the bright blue garb of the Unchurch clergy, saluted the Anti-bishop.

"We shall not be intimidated by the abuse and neglect of a hateful god!" declared the Anti-bishop. "We shall create our own rain, a generous rain of coins to bring shame to the miserly rain god. We shall prove to the Nameless one that we are better than him! Go, ride through the Poor Quarter and show how the Unchurch makes it rain!"

The rider stirred the horse, and with a clatter of hooves, it left the sanctuary by the main entrance. From outside came cheers from the crowd of commoners who had not been invited to the festival. They knew what to expect, and were prepared to form a parade behind the charity horse, and collect coins from the streets of the Poor Quarter.

The Anti-bishop called for the attention of the congregation once more. "We shall now perform a pageant of blasphemy to insult the Nameless Rain-god!"

Ushers carried in a number of shoulder-high portable partitions. These were arranged in a rough square blocking off an area in between the Anti-bishop and the congregation.

From the side gallery pranced a dozen nude men, wearing nothing but blue-and-white headdresses that resembled stylized clouds.

The nude men filed into the partitioned area, and stood within it, their nakedness now hidden, but their cloud hats splendidly visible.

From somewhere high above, a skylight slowly opened in the roof of the Grand Sanctuary. Sunlight spilled down directly into the partitioned square.

The Anti-bishop shouted, "Behold, Nameless one, this blasphemy against you!"

"BEHOLD THIS BLASPHEMY!" echoed the congregation in unison.

The cloud-headed men ducked down in unison, and were lost from view behind the partitions.

"This concludes our Rain Festival service!" said the Anti-bishop. "Please take time to greet your neighbors. Refreshments are available outside the main doors. Feel free to come up and view the blasphemy," he waggled his outstretched finger, "but don't linger too long, it would be unseemly!"

There was a general cheerful murmur from the congregation, as people got up and started moving towards the exits. Most were headed towards the main entrance and the refreshments. A few went to the front to peer over the partition and see the blasphemy.

Segna watched a pair of high priests of the Seekers of Rest approach the partition, and a moment later, they were hurrying away whispering to one another and giggling. Segna couldn't help but be a little curious.

Many of the people in the crowd seemed to want to stop and pay their respects to the King, and a knot of well-wishers rapidly formed, blocking the aisle and crowding her advisors.

"Nope," the Chief Admonisher enjoined forcefully, "This won't do at all. You can't flock Her Majesty like this. Break it up, move it out."

The Admonisher grabbed a passing acolyte. "You, organize these people outside in the square. Line them up in two neat rows, and King Segna will smile graciously at them as she walks out."

As the advisors began to orchestrate her exit, and debate whether or not to invite the Anti-bishop to walk beside her, Segna slipped away from them and headed towards the sun-drenched partition.

She stretched on her toes, and looked over the barrier to see what exactly the pageant of blasphemy really was.

"Oh!" she gasped, and averted her eyes, feeling her cheeks flush with embarrassment, but her eyes were drawn back for a second look. The Anti-bishop had been right that lingering felt unseemly, but it was still quite a sight, and difficult not to take one more glance...

# Glance

Catt and Lemmy had sat in a corner of the Great Sanctuary, among the other invited guests from the smaller temples of the city. Catt had enjoyed the show. The sermon was a lot more negative than anything Lemmy ever delivered, but it was still interesting.

Catt had taken special interest in the collection of alms. She didn't believe for an instant that all that money would end up in the hands of the poor, but she was intrigued by the execution of the scam. She was sure they would have switched the horse's saddlebags, but how was it done with so many witnesses from every angle? Perhaps the baskets were part of the trick. She would have loved to examine one of them and see if it contained some sort of a hidden mechanism or enchantment to separate and retain the more valuable Shmouds while letting the copper Thorbs pour out.

After the service had ended, Lemmy was distracted with handshakes and greetings to various other high priests, so Catt had wandered towards the front of the sanctuary.

Catt peered over the corner of the partitioned off area.

"Huh," Catt said to herself, surveying what passed for blasphemy in the Unchurch.

She looked up, and realized that a familiar face was looking in from the far side of the partitions. King Segna was standing there, eyebrows raised, her dark cheeks faintly blushing.

Segna looked up, seeing Catt, and their eyes locked together.

Catt had carefully avoided staring at the King throughout the service. As much as she had wanted to, it had been easy to avoid staring because of the fact that Catt's own seat had been nearly as far away from the King's throne as it was possible to be and still be in the same sanctuary.

Catt hadn't wanted to think about how beautiful Segna was. She hadn't wanted to think about splendidly Segna's body filled out the blue gown. She hadn't wanted to think about how Segna had held her hands on that day– how long ago had that been? More than a month– but she could still remember the softness and warmth of Segna's hands, and now they were looking directly at each other from across a square of moving skin and clouds, and it was no longer possible for Catt to avoid thinking about the feelings she had been avoiding.

Catt became aware that she was still staring into Segna's eyes, and Segna was still looking back, as if they were both frozen in time. She felt embarrassed and tried to think of how to retreat with her dignity intact. She wanted to run away without literally turning and running away. All that Catt managed was a lurching step sideways without breaking eye contact.

This motion did seem to unfreeze them, and a moment later, somehow Segna was walking towards Catt, coming around the side of the partitioned area. Segna was still looking at her, and... she was smiling.

In the time it took to draw three breaths, they were standing so close that if Catt had reached out her arms, she could almost have wrapped them around Segna. The thought sent Catt's heart beating.

Catt felt happy that she had not run away, but she also had no idea what to do or say next.

"Hello, Catt Zago," said the King.

"Hi," Catt said, biting her own lower lip.

They were now standing close enough together that staring into each other's eyes felt awkward. Catt's eyes wandered, trying to find a place to point.

And then they were standing shoulder to shoulder staring at the pageant of blasphemy again.

"What do you think?" Segna asked.

Catt thrilled at the sensation of their arms brushing together, but she managed to focus on the question. "I think... I wouldn't want to be in there, it's not my style, but I respect their... enthusiasm," Catt answered carefully.

"I agree with you entirely," Segna replied warmly. "It's not what I expected to see today... but it has a certain artistry to it."

The sound of Segna's voice talking so casually made Catt feel more comfortable.

The clouds and their attached bodies moved in the sunlight.

"I wonder why," Catt speculated, "Why do they assume that the rain god doesn't like this?"

Segna glanced upwards at the skylight and giggled.

"Maybe he's into this. If he is Nameless and silent and doesn't respond to prayers, how would they really know one way or another?"

After a moment, they both turned away from the blasphemy, and looked at each other again.

Catt suddenly felt a lump in her throat.

It must have shown in her face somehow, because Segna's expression radiated gentle sympathy, and she said. "I'm sorry I left you so suddenly last time we met."

The sensation in Catt's throat intensified and she swallowed with difficulty.

"I'm glad to see you again," Segna said.

Catt couldn't get any words out, but she managed to nod vigorous agreement.

Their moment was interrupted as an important-looking person approached from behind Segna.

"Your Majesty, it is time to withdraw from the sanctuary. To linger would be *unseemly*," the person said. This last word was delivered with a scowl towards Catt.

"Of course, Visor, thank you," said Segna, and then to Catt, "Please excuse me, Ms Zago, I must go, but I would love to see you again. If it would please you, come to the palace sometime and dine with me. You have my royal invitation."

Then she turned and walked away. The Visor raised an eyebrow curiously at Catt, but then followed Segna without another word.

Catt watched the departing King's hips swivel. She closed her open mouth, and breathed deeply, thinking about what had just happened.

After a moment, she looked around the room for where Lemmy might be. She didn't see him, but she did see an acolyte of the Unchurch approaching, already making shooing hand motions as if trying to brush her towards the door.

"Unseeeeemly!" the acolyte whispered loudly.

## Tea

Catt knocked loudly on her Landlady's half-open door. She couldn't see the old woman through the gap, but the knock elicited a response from deeper in the apartment.

"Coming, coming."

The old woman's face appeared, framed by her snowy hair and crowned by her velvety antlers.

"Hello, Ms Bethen," Catt said. "I brought you the rent."

"Ms Zago! Please come in dearie! Take some tea with me."

Catt entered, and gave Ms Bethen the coins for this week.

There was a round slate table with two chairs and two placemats. Catt made herself comfortable in one chair.

Ms Bethen busied herself finding cups and saucers. "How has life been treating you, dearie?" She asked.

Catt spied the jar of cold-brew tea by the window, and got up to fetch it. This was not the first time she had been invited to have tea with her Landlady, and she knew the routine.

"Well enough, thank you," Catt answered, bringing the jar to the table. "I feel healthy, and I'm enjoying my work."

"That is good," said Ms Bethen, placing the cups and working the jar lid. "And how is your spiritual life?"

Catt understood this to be a follow-up to their conversation from last week, when Catt had shared some of the things she had been reading about recently.

Catt replied, "I'm still learning. There are so many gods, and even when you focus on one, there seem to be so many ways of thinking about them."

Ms Bethen poured the tea. It looked brown in the jar, but took on a faint greenish hue in the cups. "What about your own goddess, dearie?"

"I still don't know if she sees me or not," Catt said. "One of my fruit seeds sprouted this week. I've been giving them water before I add the tincture, like you suggested."

"Sugar?" Ms Bethen asked.

"Just a little," Catt said.

Ms Bethen added more than just a little sugar to Catt's cup. Catt didn't complain. She took the offered spoon, but just set it aside rather than stirring.

Ms Bethen added even more sugar to her own cup, and then stirred studiously, with an expert steady hand that rarely allowed the spoon to ring against the porcelain.

"How is your love life, dearie?"

Catt stopped with the cup almost to her lips. This was a new question. She had been expecting Ms Bethen to launch into the usual report of neighborhood gossip.

Catt returned the cup to the saucer. It was the sort of question that she normally would have brushed aside, or maybe even answered flippantly, but instead she felt as if the question was like a breath, rekindling the ember of ache in her chest. Catt found that she wanted desperately to talk about it. She hadn't told anyone about the King's invitation. She hadn't even mentioned it to Lemmy.

Ms Bethen put down her spoon, and holding the cup with both hands, looked keenly at Catt over the rim.

Catt looked down at the surface of her own tea. It rippled gently as her fingers touched her cup.

"I... ran into someone I fancy a few days ago," Catt admitted. "She invited me to dinner."

"Ah!" Ms Bethen smiled. "Did you go?"

"Not yet..." Catt said.

"Oh? When is it?" Ms Bethen pried.

Catt looked away at the window. "It wasn't for any specific day," Catt said.

"Hmm..." Ms Bethen sipped her tea, and then declared, "An open invitation is serious! It means this person is not dining with anyone else. She is waiting for you."

Catt looked back at the old woman. "Does it mean that?" Catt said.

"Oh, indeed it does, dearie," said Ms Bethen with a level of confidence that Catt thought was unwarranted.

Catt shrugged a little and took hold of her tea again.

"But how long will she wait? That is harder to say. How do you feel if you wait too long and the door is closed for you?"

Catt finally tasted the tea. It was good– strong, but not bitter. "I guess I would regret it."

"Regret, young one, is a terrible thing to have in your past," said Ms Bethen, shaking her head slowly. "But regret in your future can be an asset. Knowing it is ahead of you means you can see the way to avoid it."

Catt's eyes had been wandering, but at this, she looked directly at Ms Bethen.

Ms Bethen continued. "I've a few regrets in my past, but so many more that I managed to sidestep, sometimes quite narrowly." She was smiling a little, as if taking pride in this fact.

"Maybe I should go and meet her..." Catt conceded.

# Trunks

Catt peered into the closet. It contained three big wooden trunks, stacked one on top of the other. They took up almost the whole width of the closet. In the space above the highest one was a rod for hanging clothes, but it was empty.

"Coat hangers disagree with me," explained Ms Bethen, gently touching a prong of her antlers with one hand.

Catt hefted one of the trunks out of the closet and onto the floor. Ms Bethen opened the latch.

In Catt's imagination, she had anticipated a musty-smelling jumble of old faded things, but instead the lid lifted to reveal perfectly folded garments in bright and vivid colors. The air suddenly smelled like lavender and snow.

"I was your size when I was younger," said Ms Bethen. "I think most of these will fit you."

Catt picked up a red and purple dress from the top, and sniffed it deeply. "How do these smell so good?"

Ms Bethen chuckled, "Back in those days, my dear, I could afford to buy enchanted perfumes that would keep things fresh. It was a good investment for theater work. You can get quite sweaty on the stage, with no chance for washing between shows."

Catt unfolded the dress and held it up to herself. "It's really not my style though," she said, and began to re-fold it, conscious that she was not doing a very good job of it.

Ms Bethen took it from Catt and placed it on the table. "Don't worry," she said, "We'll find you something you can wear to dine with your friend."

For a while they sorted through the chest, Ms Bethen sometimes relating stories that the dresses reminded her of.

"These are beautiful," Catt said, "but I don't like wearing dresses, I like trousers. What if I have to climb? What if I have to sprint?"

"At a romantic dinner? Sprinting?"

Catt shrugged.

"Tell me, dearie, what were you wearing the first time this friend of yours ever saw you?"

Catt looked down at herself. "I was dressed like this... mostly. I also had my coat and my sword."

Ms Bethen nodded and scratched her chin. "I've never seen you with a sword, dearie."

"I sold it," Catt lied quickly.

"Very well, a new approach then. Let us get out that other trunk."

Once the second trunk had been removed from the closet, it was opened to reveal a considerably more eclectic mix of garments. Like the contents of the other trunk, they smelled wonderful, but these defied being neatly folded. There were more unusual designs and a mixture of mundane and exotic materials. A few stage props that were not garments at all were mixed in.

Catt lifted what appeared to be a small ornate sleeveless white shirt. "What is this?" she asked, examining the bottom edge which was irregularly frayed.

"That's the bodice half of a dress. It was for a fairy bride part that I played. I cut off the skirt part and re-used it on another dress. I don't think I still have that one. I kept the bodice because I liked the lace-work so much."

Catt clutched the bodice to her chest. "Wait, are you saying you made some of these yourself?"

"I made nearly all of them myself!" said Ms Bethen with pride. "Acting is hardly my only talent!"

Catt continued to cling to the bodice. She wanted it. With its floral lace and complicated neckline and artfully asymmetrical shoulders it was every bit as beautiful as any of the dresses in the first trunk, but it was also obviously and dramatically *not a dress*.

"I could just wear this with my own trousers..." suggested Catt.

Ms Bethen shook her head firmly. "No you can't, dearie." But then she smiled. "However, I think I know just the thing."

Ms Bethen went to the third trunk, and opened it where it sat on the floor of the closet.

The contents of this trunk had many blacks and grays, but still a few bright splashes of color as well.

She lifted up a pair of black trousers with shining metallic parts, and showed it to Catt.

"What is that?" Catt asked, intrigued.

"I made this for my late husband. They are intended to look like greaves. He was playing the lead in an adaptation of the *Seventh Brigand Warlord*, and the theater had plenty of stage armor, but all of it was too unwieldy, and he couldn't dance in it."

Catt tried to imagine what a dancing warlord would have looked like. "I wish I could have seen that," she said.

"Try them on, dearie," suggested Ms Bethen. "There is a mirror in the other room."

# Invitation

"I was invited," said Catt.

The butler stared at her.

"By the King," Catt clarified. Her voice echoed off the polished marble walls of the palace narthex.

"You can check with the Visor," she added, at the butler's continued blank silence.

She was trying to think what else she could say, when the butler finally reacted.

"Wait here, if you please." The butler turned about, and strode away through the entrance hall, shortly vanishing around a corner.

Catt was left alone in the narthex, but for the one executioner who seemed to be standing guard in the corner. Catt glared defiantly at the executioner, but he ignored her, and continued humming softly to himself and staring at the grand front doors.

"I'll just wait here then!" Catt affirmed, loudly.

Her voice echoed.

It seemed like an eternity waiting for the butler, and after a while, Catt began to imitate the humming of the executioner on guard duty. She would harmonize with him for a while, and then switch to a dissonant tune to try to throw him off, or annoy him, or get some kind of a reaction.

Finally, the butler returned, together with a person Catt recognized. It was the important-looking person that Segna had referred to as "Visor" at the Rain Festival.

Catt smiled politely at them.

"This is Ms Catt Zago," said the butler to the Visor. "She asserts that she was invited by the King."

"Yes, so nice to see you again, Visor," Catt said, giving a little bow.

The Visor looked her over appraisingly, with an air of curiosity mixed with undisguised disgust.

"I do not recognize this flamboyant reprobate," snapped the Visor, turning their back on Catt and addressing the butler, "When you waste my time, you waste Her Majesty's time."

Catt hadn't expected a warm welcome, but she was shocked to have been so firmly rebuffed.

With a swishing of cloaks, the Visor scurried away. The butler was left nonplussed, staring at Catt.

"I'm sorry, I cannot allow you in," said the butler after a moment's awkward silence.

"What if I just go in anyway?" Catt asked, letting a hint of menace drip into her voice.

The executioner in the corner cleared his throat loudly. Catt glanced over at him, he was still staring absently at the doors, but his axe had moved quietly from his belt to his hand.

Catt took a step backwards away from the butler. "I think there has been a mistake," she said.

"It seems so," the butler agreed.

Catt seethed numbly as she retreated from the palace. Outside, on the terraced area in front of the palace, she turned and looked up at the massive building. From this close, the mountains behind it were dwarfed and swallowed up by the building's profile.

Catt felt hopeless and defeated– but yet– beneath her belly full of frustration was a hard kernel of stubbornness. She didn't doubt for a minute the sincerity of Segna's invitation, rather, she placed the blame squarely on the Visor.

Did Segna know? Catt wondered, did she know that her advisors were intentionally isolating her? If she didn't know, then she ought to be told. Then a thought occurred to Catt. What if Segna *did* know she was being isolated, and had invited Catt to dinner because she needed help.

Catt was still looking at the towering palace, but it was no longer the gaze of someone defeated looking upon the place of her defeat, now she was looking at the edifice with the eyes of a problem solver, searching for another way in.

Clearly, the palace had been built with aesthetics in mind, not security. Catt could spot a dozen climbing paths that could potentially lead to balconies and open windows on the upper levels, but unfortunately none of them were concealed. Being able to scale the building would do her no good if she had to do it in full sight of everyone in the whole city square.

Catt circled around towards the left side of the palace, hoping to case the whole circumference of the building, and perhaps find a more favorable route for sneaking in.

# Badge

The back of the palace nestled right up to the craggy foothills of the mountains. Zig-zagging staircases were cut into the stones, some leading upwards to terraces in the foothills where there were other buildings, much smaller than the palace, but by the look of them they were still mansions for nobles and lords.

One broad staircase led to what appeared to be a servant's entrance on the rearmost wall of the palace. Catt could see people moving up and down it, carrying things, going about palace business.

She felt she would be conspicuous standing there at the bottom of the stairs, casing the entrance, so she retreated, returning to the front of the palace, and seated herself on a marble bench underneath one of the trees in the square. This seemed like a popular place for people to linger, and she felt she could loiter here without attracting attention. She spent some time watching to see who was going to or coming from around the left side of the palace. After a bit of observation, she began to be able to characterize the typical sorts of people who seemed to be using the palace's rear entrance.

There were servants and cleaners, and a few people who looked like craftspersons, carrying tools or paints. There were also occasionally some executioners, which suggested to Catt that they served as palace guards. The grim irony of their being the King's protectors while at the same time being destined to be her murderers galled Catt's sensibilities, but she put those thoughts aside.

The main type of person using the rear entrance were porters. She watched them going back and forth, wearing the white sleeveless uniform with the yellow and orange badge of the Cook's Guild, and carrying big baskets and covered trays and pairs of bags on shoulder-yokes.

The Cook's Guild Porters accounted for more than half of all the persons she observed that were moving in the direction she cared about. It made sense that fine food would be brought to the palace, after all, the Unburning curse meant that kitchens inside the palace would be useless. The large number of porters suggested to Catt that this wasn't simply for the King's table, rather there were probably quite a lot of important and hungry people in the palace at any given time.

What if the King was holding some kind of a banquet today? Catt wondered if today might be a uniquely bad day for her to be sneaking in to keep a dinner date, but then again, maybe this was just a normal afternoon, and maybe there were always that many porters. Perhaps they even delivered other things besides food? Could they also serve as the city's Royal Mail? Porters delivering messages was actually rather less of a stretch than executioners serving as guards.

As Catt was watching and pondering, she suddenly realized that one of the people she was watching was watching her back.

A man wearing a porter's uniform was making eye contact with her. His ears and lower lip were covered in silvery rings and studs. Catt recognized the man she had knocked down in the Smokefields a few weeks past.

The man had clearly already recognized her. Hatred was gleaming in his eyes, and he changed direction and began approaching her.

Catt could feel her heart beat faster, but she forced a charade of calm.

"You!" spat the man, "Don't think for a minute that I forgot about you!" He reached a point a few paces away from Catt's bench and stopped.

Catt affected confusion. "I'm sorry. Do I know you?"

"*Unlicensed carrier!*" growled the man, the words dripping with spite as if this was the worst obscenity he knew how to voice.

"What's your problem?" Catt asked, holding out her empty hands. "I'm not carrying nothing."

"I ought to give you the beating I owe you!" said the man, taking a step closer.

Catt rested her elbows on the back of the bench with calculated nonchalance. "Really? You're gonna attack me? Right here In the square?"

His bluff was called. She could see his eyes shifting quickly back and forth, and taking in the number of witnesses.

"I'll get you," he said menacingly, "When you least expect it. Next time you won't see me coming."

He turned his back abruptly and walked away.

"Okay, nice chat! Bye!" Catt mocked.

She watched him leave the square as she assembled the rest of her plan in her head.

The moment the man disappeared around the corner of a distant building, she was up, and hurrying in the same direction.

Catt was almost at a run when she reached the street that he had gone down. She caught sight of his back in the distance, and dropped back to a walk.

She tailed the man all the way out of Old Bakak, and into the Marketday district, closing the distance carefully, but keeping far enough back to avoid notice. He showed no sign of suspecting that he was being followed.

Catt guessed that the man was heading for the Smokefields, and she figured she had to act before he reached Sausage Row, with its heavy foot traffic.

When she saw him turn down a relatively deserted side street, she made her move.

Catt sprinted, closing the distance between herself and the man in a matter of seconds. She pounced with all her momentum, while simultaneously grabbing at his shirt. The clean execution of this surprise maneuver was essential to the success of her attack.

A lone passer-by yelped at the sight of her tackle, and the man, alerted, started to turn about, but he was too late. As Catt collided with him, she dragged his whole shirt upwards towards his neck. His arms went up, both to defend against Catt's onslaught, and to defend against his impact with the ground.

As they both crashed into the ground together, skidding and scraping across the street, Catt rolled right over him, and dragged his shirt completely inside-out over his head. For an instant he was blinded and his arms were entangled, and Catt managed to land a couple of vicious blows to his torso with her knee before he wriggled out of his shirt entirely, and rolled clear of her.

In an instant he was on his feet again, center of gravity low, fists clenched, muscles coiled, ready to fight back and fight hard.

Catt barely saw this, because she was already hightailing it away from him, fleeing with all the swiftness of a wild rabbit.

"Yeah, you better run!" shouted the man. "You better run, Coward!"

Catt noted the triumphant tone to his shouts. He believed he had won. He believed that his dexterity had saved him from a mugging, and that his ferocity had frightened away his foolish attacker.

Catt left him behind as she rounded a corner. A joyous grin was stretched over her face. She had won. The gambit had worked perfectly. She had gotten away without a scratch, and she still had the shirt in her hand– the white shirt with its beautifully embroidered official Cook's Guild Porter's badge on the right breast.

# Basket

Catt turned randomly down side streets, unsure if she was being pursued. After a few minutes, she spotted a shop on a corner with two open doors, one facing each street. She stepped inside. This would be a good place to wait. If the man caught up with her, it would be difficult for him to corner her.

The shop seemed to sell every sort of woven thing from tapestries to hammocks. Catt pretended to be browsing the wares. She had rolled up the shirt and wrapped it in a knot around her wrist.

After a few more minutes, Catt was sufficiently confident that she had shaken her pursuer– if he had even actually pursued.

Catt spotted a shelf with some wicker baskets. They looked similar to what a porter might use to carry food. She picked out a medium sized one, big enough to look plausible, but small enough to not be cumbersome.

Catt toyed with the idea of stealing it, but decided that she had already been lucky enough, and she didn't need to push that luck any further with unnecessary risks.

She paid a few Thorbs to the shopkeeper, and left with the basket.

Stopping in the shadow of a stairwell on the side of another shop, Catt unrolled the shirt, and pulled it on over the top of her not-a-dress bodice. It smelled faintly of sweat and smoke. Her dancing greaves were hardly an ideal match for the porter's disguise, but based on her previous observations, she concluded that the flame-shaped guild badge was the most important part, followed by the basket. Nobody was likely to take excessive notice of her rather unusual trousers.

Hefting the basket, Catt continued walking briskly back towards the palace.

Realizing that if she held the basket in her arms it would obscure her badge, Catt switched to balancing the basket on her head, as she had seen some porters doing. The tapered base of the basket nestled nicely between her little horns, which gave it stability, but she kept one hand on it anyway, to add to the illusion that it was heavier than it really was.

Catt walked with the purposeful stride of someone who had to bring a hot delicacy directly to the King before it had time to cool.

When she reached the square of Old Bakak, she headed unhesitatingly for the back of the palace.

Spotting a couple other porters with baskets, she adjusted her pace to follow close enough behind them that she could imitate their entry.

Up the stone steps, a sharp turn, and in through the archway of the door. An executioner was posted there, sitting on a stool, but they seemed to be paying little attention to the porters who preceded Catt, and a moment later, Catt was inside the palace, having been accosted by nothing more than a polite nod from the wooden mask.

She followed the other porters, hopefully towards wherever the meals were being staged for presentation to whoever was dining at whatever meal the King might be hosting.

# Guest

The dining hall of King Segna's palace was spacious, but it only contained one table.

Functionally it was just one table, but it was modular, being extended by pushing together numerous triangular table segments, and concealing the seams between their smooth stone tops with an overlapping mosaic of multiple vibrant tablecloths.

The table sometimes seemed to Segna as if it was an amorphous living thing, changing in size and shape each time she saw it, ever-changing in spite of its stony solidity.

At times when she dined with her advisors, there would only be a dozen or so seats arrayed around it, but today, it sprawled out further than usual, to accommodate the Near-Shoming trade delegation, and the local lords and guildmasters who were here to mingle with them.

King Segna had already endured a tedious and grueling tariff negotiation session with them all day long, and was feeling most relieved that her only remaining part to play was that of social host.

The guildmasters could have them now and do with them whatever they wished for all she cared.

The first course had already been served, and Segna was idly nibbling on grilled sweet root sprouts while listening to the Visor of Protocol arguing with the Chief Admonisher, which pleased her because it meant that neither of them was talking to her.

Servants were moving about the room, both her own servants, and the ones who were part of the retinue of the Near-Shomings. The hall was full of a general murmur of conversation and clinking of silver and porcelain. A servant topped off Segna's glass of wine, and she reached for it.

Something tapped on Segna's knee.

She started, nearly spilling the wine, and might have jumped entirely out of her seat, except that something about the gentleness of the unexpected touch seemed to be a communication.

Segna scooted backwards, and peered under the hanging corner of the tablecloth.

A face was peering back at her. It winked.

It was the face of Ms Catt Zago, that same woman whom Segna had met on the day of her own coronation, and again, not so long ago, at the Rain Festival.

Segna remembered inviting the outlandish but attractive Catt to come to the palace and dine with her, and now, quite unheralded, here she was, appearing in such a bold way that it was positively ridiculous.

Segna looked around to see if anyone else had noticed, but her advisors were still arguing and eating.

She wanted to ask, "What in the name of all that is magical are you doing down there!?" But she did not say this because she did not wish to alert those sitting nearest to her. She wasn't sure how they would react– in fact, she really wasn't sure how she should react herself.

Segna took a deep breath and let it out slowly to clear her thoughts, and she realized that even above surprise and confusion, the emotion that she was feeling most strongly was elation. A moment before she had been eating dinner in a room full of people who she did not wish to spend a single moment more time with, and now suddenly that was no longer true. She was glad that Catt had answered her invitation, no matter how strangely she had done it.

Segna scooted a little closer to the table, and reached one hand under the tablecloth, meaning to take hold of Catt's hand and squeeze it. Instead she found that she was touching Catt's face. Catt was pressing a cheek gently against Segna's palm. She could feel her fingertips brush against the soft lobe of Catt's ear.

Segna felt her own cheeks grow hot, and she looked around her again, wondering self consciously if anyone else was noticing what was going on. Nobody was. Everyone else at the table seemed absorbed in their food or in their neighbors.

Segna crossed her legs. Having a dinner guest, even a very welcome one, between her knees felt decidedly indecorous. As intriguing as the situation was, it was no way to share a meal.

Raising her free hand, Segna gestured for a passing servant. "Fetch me another chair," she commanded.

The servant gave a mutedly quizzical look, but said, "Right away your majesty."

Segna felt Catt's jaw nodding, as if acknowledging that she understood. The smooth skin of her cheek slipped away, and Segna was unsure where her hidden guest was.

The servant returned bearing a spare chair.

"Put it here beside me," Segna instructed, moving her own chair slightly to the side.

The servant obediently placed the chair in the gap between Segna and the Visor of Protocol, who was still hotly engaged in debate, and had their back half turned on her.

"Please set another place here," Segna asked of the servant.

Segna regained her fork and took another bite of the root sprouts. She felt excited anticipation, trying not to look at the empty seat beside her.

Far across the table, she caught a wide-eyed expression of amusement on the face of one of the Near-Shoming ambassadors who was looking her way.

Segna looked to her side, and the chair was now occupied by her new dinner companion, staring back at her and smiling.

"I'm pleased that you could join me," Segna said.

"The pleasure is all mine," Catt replied with a grin.

The servant returned an instant later, and without expressing any surprise, began setting out Catt's plate.

Segna noticed that Catt was dressed far more nicely than when they had met before. She was wearing something white with lace, and although Segna prevented herself from gazing in an undignified manner, it seemed to her peripheral vision that Catt was wearing plates of form-fitting armor on her legs.

The second course was now being served.

After their congenial greeting, Segna volunteered no further small talk, waiting to see what conversation Catt would offer. Although she was delighted by the appearance of her company, she was also aware that to sneak into a King's dining hall under the table was extremely presumptuous, and she was aware that they were being watched. The wide-eyed diplomat across the table was hardly the only person to have taken notice of the sudden and unconventional arrival of the new guest.

Before Segna had a chance to discover what banter her bold friend might be ready to engage in, the Visor of Protocol, distracted from their argument by the arrival of the meat, realized that they were no longer seated closest to the King.

"How in the hells–" they started, looking shocked.

"Hi!" Catt said. She seemed pleased by the Visor's reaction, her expression mischievous.

"I should!– well– I never!" sputtered the Visor of Protocol. "How did this person get here, your Majesty?" they demanded.

"This is Ms Zago," Segna said demurely. "You remember Ms Zago? I invited her."

The Visor's face turned red with anger, and Segna noted how odd it seemed that the Visor was reacting so strongly. Perhaps they simply disliked surprises?

The Chief Admonisher seemed delighted that the Visor was so discomfited. "Come now, Old Protocol!" they said with a grin. "Don't be rude to the King's guest!" The Admonisher reached impertinently across the Visor's plate to offer a hand to Catt. "So nice to make your acquaintance!" they said.

"Enchanted," said Catt, touching the Admonisher's hand serenely.

The Visor trembled, apparently unable to manage the same sort of pleasantry.

"I can go, if I am intruding," Catt said to the Visor, beginning to rise from the chair.

Segna took hold of Catt's arm. Catt was certainly intruding, but Segna certainly didn't want her to go.

The Visor's eyes fell on Segna's hand, taking in the overly-intimate action. Comprehension seemed to dawn in their face.

"Nonsense," said the Visor, regaining their professional composure, "I forget myself. Please forgive me, your Majesty. Of course... Ms Zago... is welcome. Far be it from me to impinge upon the King's hospitality."

Catt settled back into her seat, and Segna let go of her arm, embarrassed to have been so unsubtle.

## Dinner Magic

Catt Zago ate dinner with the King. It seemed surreal, but it was happening.

After the momentary squabble with the Visor, the advisors largely left them alone. The other important-looking people at the table, whoever they were, gawked at them at first, but Catt found them increasingly easy to ignore as she focused her attention on Segna.

They talked about the food, and how good it was, and complemented one another on their wardrobes, and spent some moments in comfortable silence, simply savoring the flavors of their meals in proximity to one another.

"What have you been doing with yourself since we first met?" Segna asked Catt.

"I've been working as an acolyte at a temple," Catt said.

"I thought I remembered you saying you were in the business of causing trouble?" Segna asked, "Isn't that quite a change of career?"

Catt felt pleased that Segna had remembered this detail. "It *is* rather different than what I am used to," Catt admitted, "but I like it. And it is not as if I have to give up on trouble entirely– I am here, aren't I?"

Segna smiled, but kept on topic. "What god? What temple?" asked the King.

"It's the Polypantheonic Temple," Catt replied.

"I don't know that one," said Segna.

"It's for worshiping practically *all* the gods… at least, all except the major ones who already have big temples of their own."

A ripple of recognition ran across Segna's face. "Oh! I had heard there was a temple like that, I suppose I just didn't know anything about it."

"What about you?" Catt asked. "How does your new job compare to teaching young wizards?"

Catt thought that Segna's eyes became distant for a moment, but then she shook it off and answered.

"I can eat like this," Segna gestured at the plate, "And live like that," Segna gestured upwards.

Catt guessed the gesture was meant to indicate the whole palace.

"And I do have the power to change things for the better… even if that takes time… But…" Segna faltered, "I do miss working with magic."

"Can't you still do it?" Catt asked. "It seems like magic would be a valuable skill for a King, isn't it?"

"There haven't been that many opportunities," said Segna.

"Can you cast a spell to silence your Visor when they get quippy?" Catt asked in a conspiratorial whisper.

A smile crooked Segna's lips as she shook her head no. "I have to work with these people. That would just make them even more 'quippy', as you put it, when the ward of silence wore off."

"But you actually *could* do a spell like that?" Catt put down her fork and rested her elbow on the table and her chin on her hand.

"I could do that one from a book, I don't have it memorized. It takes a lot of work to commit a spell to memory in a useful form."

"What can you do from memory?" Catt asked.

"Well," Segna took a small bite from her plate and chewed thoughtfully. Swallowing, she said, "Give me your glass."

Catt picked up the long stemmed glass which still contained a little wine. She handed it to Segna.

Segna held it gingerly with the fingertips of one hand. "This one is easy, because it is very small, and I am doing it at close range."

"Okay, ready!" Catt said, delighted.

Segna began to mutter a string of syllables. Some of it was unintelligible, but Catt thought she recognized a few of the words. She thought she heard the Arashan verbs for "turning" and "drawing out", but Segna spoke quickly, and it was hard to tell.

Suddenly the glass shattered, fragments raining loudly onto each of their plates. A big chunk fell hard on the table. Segna's hand flinched, and she dropped the still intact stem.

"Oh! Oh! I'm sorry!" Segna cried, sounding shaken.

Catt reached for Segna, "Are you alright?" She was concerned that Segna's hand might have been cut by the glass.

Segna laughed. "I'm so sorry!" she repeated. She didn't seem hurt. "I shouldn't have done it that way!"

"Are you sure you are okay?" Catt had taken ahold of Segna's hand and was inspecting it. There was no blood visible.

"It worked, look!" said Segna, pointing at the table with the other hand.

On the table, besides the shards of the glass, there was a small purple object between the plates.

It took Catt a moment to realize what it was. It was the wine, still perfectly matching the shape of the glass where it had rested before.

Catt reached out and picked it up, yelped, dropped it, and then picked it up again. It was icy cold in her fingers, frozen solid.

"I usually did that with metal tumblers when I did it in class," explained Segna. "I forgot about the effect the cold would have on the glass. I'm so sorry." This last apology was directed to the servant who had just arrived at her side and was sweeping up the fragments of glass.

"It's nothing, your Majesty," insisted the servant.

Catt observed that most of the conversation in the room had stopped. Some people were standing, as if to get a better view.

"There's a piece on my plate too," said the Visor, sourly to the servant.

"I'm sorry, Visor, that was careless of me," said Segna.

"I believe I shall retire, your Majesty, good night," said the Visor, rising.

"But dessert!" protested the Admonisher, sardonically, at the Visor's receding back. "They were about to bring the dessert!"

"You should follow! Take them some!" Catt suggested.

The Admonisher grinned, "You know, I like how you think." They got up and followed the Visor, accosting a servant and raiding a dessert tray on the way out.

Catt looked at the two empty chairs next to her, and then she leaned close to Segna. "You said you couldn't do it... but your magic silenced *both* of them!"

Segna giggled. "So I did!"

Catt licked the frozen chunk of wine which was beginning to melt on her chilled fingers. "It's good this way, try some," she offered the wine to Segna.

Segna rolled her eyes, but she was smiling.

"Can you show me another spell?" Asked Catt.

"I really shouldn't," Segna said, looking around at the other guests. "Would... would you like to go somewhere else where we can talk more?"

"I would like that very much," said Catt.

# Dessert

Catt followed Segna up a spiral of green marble stairs. She was carrying two small dessert plates laden with large slices of honey carob cake.

They reached a higher floor, passed through a few archways, and stopped in front of a pair of double doors opposite a balcony. Segna put her hands on the handles and pushed.

Inside were three more steps up. Catt's eyes were on Segna as she climbed them. She followed, butterfly wings in her stomach.

The room was wide and rounded. Half of it was a balcony looking out over the rooftops of Old Bakak. The night sky was at that shade of dark blue that lingers for only a few moments before it turns black. The other side of the room had several openings, branching into other rooms. Magic lanterns mounted on the walls gave off a cold steady light that was very unlike candlelight. It was not bright.

Segna removed her slippers and left them near the entrance. Catt followed suit, removing her boots.

There was a small table near the center of the balcony which was dwarfed by an oversized plush chair. Catt placed the dessert plates on the table.

Segna was fetching a stool from another part of the room. "I'm sorry I only have these little seats that the advisors use sometimes." She sat on the edge of the big chair, as if self consciously avoiding leaning back into its spacious seat.

Catt sat on the stool.

"That looks big enough for two!" said Catt, grinning.

Segna bit her lip, seemed to take a slow breath, and then scooted sideways.

Catt moved and joined Segna in the big chair, leaving the stool abandoned. The plush chair was very soft, and the seat was big enough that they could both sit side by side without pressing their hips together. There was air between them, but only just a little.

"You wanted to know more about magic?" Segna asked quickly.

"Yes, more of that please!" said Catt, reaching for one of the plates of cake, and sampling it with the spoon.

Segna talked about magic, and Catt listened, and sometimes asked questions.

The sky darkened, and moonlight illuminated the city.

The slices of cake diminished bite by bite, but neither vanished completely. They were very large slices.

After a while, Segna went to fetch one of her books of magic from another room. When she returned, and sat, the air space between them was gone. They leaned against each other with the large volume open over both their knees as Segna showed Catt planar focus diagrams, and illustrations of various hand gestures.

"Can you teach me to do a spell?" asked Catt. "Something simple?"

"We could try a spell for beginners," Segna said, flipping to a page close to the beginning.

"Is this what you would have taught new students on their first day in class?" Catt asked.

"No," Segna said with a laugh, "This is what they would have learned from some other teacher in an entry-level classroom *years* before they ever got to my class."

"Okay, that sounds about right for me," Catt said.

They studied the simple spell, and Segna explained each component.

"I know some of these words," Catt said, as Segna was coaching her through memorization of the verbal part of the spell, "A lot of them sound like Arashan words, they're just spelled with the Shoming alphabet."

"Do you speak Arashan?" asked Segna curiously.

"*Quite Fluently*," Catt said in Arashan.

Segna smiled broadly, showing her beautiful teeth. "I didn't understand that, but I'll take it as a *yes*," she said. "I don't speak the language, but I know that quite a lot of the spells and magical techniques taught at the university were first invented in Arash.

Once Catt had memorized the words and the hand gestures, and had stared at the focus diagrams long enough to be able to close her eyes and still visualize the lines, Segna declared, "You are ready to try."

Segna took one of the spoons and stuck it upright, with the handle end pushed into the remains of one of the slices of cake.

Catt looked at her distorted reflection in the spoon.

"Okay, knock it down," Segna instructed.

Catt held her left hand in the first position. She imagined the intersecting lines of the focus. She began to speak the words of the spell Segna had taught her. As she pronounced the syllables, she moved her hand through the three positions of the gesture.

As she spoke the final word, the spoon languidly flopped over, hitting the table with an anticlimactic thunk.

"You did it!" exclaimed Segna, clapping.

Catt spoke the last stanza of the spell again, this time replacing the verb for "fall down" with the verb for "rise up". As she did this, she reversed the hand gestures, and imagined the lines of the focus tugging the spoon back upright.

There was a sharp *ping*, and the spoon shot spinning towards the ceiling, scattering cake crumbs. It struck the smooth stone above, and ricocheted over the balcony to vanish into the night.

"Oh! Catt!" Segna grabbed Catt's hand and forcefully closed it into a fist. "Don't!"

"I didn't really think that would work!" beamed Catt, pleased with herself.

"Please don't improvise like that!" Segna pleaded, "That was so dangerous! Changing a spell like that can be incredibly unpredictable!"

Catt nodded, understanding the gravity that Segna was trying to communicate, but Catt was still unable to wipe the grin off her face. She felt so happy. She had done magic, but even more than that, she was happy because Segna was there, caring about her, clasping her hand tightly, her face just inches away and full of concern.

"Please don't take risks like that for nothing!" Segna was saying.

"I'm sorry," Catt said, honestly, "I promise I won't take risks for no reason."

"Good," Segna said, "Please, please, please don't make me regret teaching you that." She looked into Catt's eyes. Her grip softened, but she didn't let go of Catt's hand.

"I promise to only take risks when I have a very good reason," Catt continued.

Segna looked like she was about to say something else, but before she did, Catt took a risk. She leaned forward, bringing her face closer to Segna's, just a breath away.

"May I?" Catt whispered.

Segna lips parted in surprise. Then she wordlessly, but firmly, nodded *"yes"*.

Their lips joined softly, for what felt like a long time, but may have been only a moment, it was hard to tell.

When the gentle exploration had completed, they moved apart a few inches and looked at each other. Catt could feel her own heart beating. She watched the way Segna drew breath deeply.

"Is this too much?" Catt queried. "Am I moving too fast?"

Segna shook her head. One more deep breath, and then she said, "No. I want this. I need this."

Catt could see the corners of Segna's eyes glistening.

As their faces grew closer together, a few more words escaped Segna's lips.

"I don't have time for moving slowly."

As they kissed a second time, the passion welling up inside Catt was tempered and made more complex by this last thought, because it made real the same anxious fear that Catt herself had been refusing to think about all evening.

# Consort

Catt woke up slowly.

It took some time for her senses to untangle waking from dreaming.

The morning light was dim and strange. The surface beneath her was too soft. There was pressure and warmth at her side. A weight was nestled into her shoulder. The soft sound of breathing.

Segna was asleep.

Catt understood where she was. Her senses continued to grow clearer.

She could make out the shape of the room in the dim light. The open archway to the next room admitting red morning sun. The magic lanterns on the walls faded away to nearly nothing.

She could smell perfumed oil, and feel the tangle of silk sheets haphazardly around her, and she could feel the gentle in and out of Segna's respiration.

Catt thought about where she was and what had happened.

Catt tried to carefully wriggle herself loose without waking up Segna, pillowed on her shoulder. She felt as if she had to get up and sneak out, and let the memory of this perfect night be self-contained. She had bedded a King. She had made love to the most beautiful woman in the city of Great Bakak. It was the perfect one night stand. She told herself that she had to leave now so she could remember it that way. She almost half believed it.

Catt gently dislodged her shoulder and sat up. She looked around the perimeter of the colossal round bed. She didn't see where her clothes had ended up. As she started to move, she felt a hand touch her.

"Catt," whispered Segna.

Catt looked back. Segna's eyes were still half closed. Catt felt as if butterflies were inside her again.

"I have to go," Catt managed to say.

"Will you come back again sometime?" Segna asked drowsily.

Catt felt a facade crumbling in her imagination. A moment ago it seemed possible to run away and preserve a perfect experience, isolated in time, and to avoid the pain of it ending.

Now maybe it was too late. If Catt said "No" she would hurt Segna and regret it forever. If Catt said "Yes" and it was a lie, she would hurt her even more.

But if she said "Yes" and it was the truth, this perfect moment could be repeated— not forever, the pain of it ending would still have to come, but it could be delayed.

"Yes," said Catt, "I'll be back some other night."

"Good," murmured Segna. She smiled and stretched and resettled and seemed to fall back asleep.

Catt found her clothes on the floor at the edge of the plateau of bed. They were folded and stacked neatly.

Catt looked back at Segna, nestled peacefully in the sheets. Had she woken in the middle of the night and tidied up?

Catt dressed quickly. She went towards the arch that was now streaming sunlight.

Through the arch and into the next room. There was the wide balcony. There was the big chair and the table. Someone had cleared away the cake plates.

Catt startled to see that there were two people in the room, one sweeping the floor, another on a stepladder polishing one of the magic lanterns on the wall. Servants apparently?

Both of them looked at her. Catt felt as if they were both grinning and leering, but in fact both of them turned back to their work without a second glance.

Catt found her boots by the door, and made a hasty exit.

On the way down the stairs, Catt encountered two of the King's advisors, on their way up. One of them was the Admonisher.

"Aha! Ms Zago! Just the person we were hoping to find!"

Catt wondered if she was going to need to run.

The Admonisher continued, "The Steward here has something for you."

The Steward extended a hand holding a necklace. It was a short chain of what looked like gold, with a heart-shaped pennant hanging from it.

"What is this?" Catt asked, confused and suspicious.

"This is a Consort's Locket," said the Steward in a serious tone that seemed to imply that this was an auspicious thing to be receiving.

"I don't... know what that is," Catt protested. She shifted sideways along the step, hoping to slip past them.

"It means you can come and go as you please, as long as you are the King's Consort," the Admonisher explained.

Catt looked at it again.

"You really should take it," they continued, "Wearing it will make it quite difficult for the Visor of Protocol to keep you out."

The Steward rolled their eyes, as if reacting to the mention of the Visor, and proffered the locket more imperatively.

Catt took it.

"Excellent," said the Steward, clearly pleased, "You may keep it until the King asks for it back, or until her execution, whichever comes first."

Catt shuddered, clutching the necklace in her fist. She squeezed past the advisors and continued down the stairs without another word.

"And thank you!" the Admonisher called after her, "We've been worried about Her Majesty! A good fuck is probably just what she needed!"

The Steward gasped slightly at this.

Catt left them behind, taking the steps two at a time. She wasn't embarrassed. She didn't care what the advisors or the servants or anyone else said about her or thought about her. The reminder of Segna's death on the other hand, gnawed at Catt. How many months did she have left? Nine? Ten? Catt had never had a romantic relationship that lasted that long. How long could a relationship between a King and a Thief last?

Catt felt committed to trying and finding out. She fastened the Consort's Locket around her neck as she walked.

# Pennies

"You look happy this morning, dearie!" declared Ms Bethen. She was sitting on the front steps of the apartment house, an embroidery hoop in her hands.

"I *feel* happy, Ms Bethen," Catt said, blushing in spite of herself. She had not told her Landlady whom she was seeing, but the old woman had taken notice of Catt's early-morning arrivals every few days for the past two weeks.

"Do stop by for tea when you have time," said Ms Bethen.

"I will, thank you," Catt said. She knew Ms Bethen was hungry for gossip. Catt waved and continued upstairs.

Reaching her room, Catt drank some of the clean water she had purified the day before. She washed her face, and gave some water to the sprouted seed on her window ledge. She would need to find soil for it soon, but that wouldn't happen today, she had things to do.

Catt looked at her bed. It looked so tiny and lonely. It was still made neatly. "I'll sleep in you tonight," she told it.

The bed did not reply.

Catt changed her clothes. She kept the Consort's Locket on. It would be hidden under her collar. She didn't need to take it with her today, it would be two more nights before she saw Segna again. Over the past two weeks she had spent five nights at the palace. A part of her yearned to go there every day, and to wake up next to Segna every morning, but she also wanted to maintain her independence. She still wanted her own life separate from being the King's Consort.

An hour later, Catt arrived at the Polypantheonic Temple. Lemmy was pouring over some of his indexes of deities and aspects, preparing for the day's appointments.

Catt had not told Lemmy anything either. Unless he happened to gossip with Ms Bethen, he probably didn't even know Catt was seeing someone.

"You're well travelled, Catt," Lemmy said. "Perhaps you can help me understand something."

"I can try," Catt offered, coming to look over Lemmy's shoulder.

"I'm reading about Saint Buster," Lemmy said.

"For the wedding this afternoon?"

"Yes," confirmed Lemmy. "The symbology keeps making reference to a *'penny'*, and I'm not quite certain what that word means. I can tell from context that it is some kind of coin, but I don't see if there is anything special about the coin, or why the writer chose to translate it phonetically instead of just saying 'coin'?"

Catt scratched her head. "I don't know about Saint Buster, but I do remember that in Srappa they have a coin called a penny. It's a little tin thing. Their smallest valued coin."

"So it is similar to a Thorb then?" asked Lemmy.

"Not really," said Catt with a shrug. "It's worth much less. I'd say you would need at least 200 pennies to buy what you could buy here with one Thorb."

"Two hundred!" Lemmy exclaimed, "how quaintly impractical!"

"I remember collecting a whole handful of them so I could buy one piece of sugar-candy when I was young." Catt gestured with her outstretched palm facing down to indicate how small she had been at that age.

"Most interesting!" said Lemmy, flipping backwards one page in his book to re-read a passage. "That puts all these coin metaphors in a different context," he pointed to a line on the page. "This one isn't a signifier of prosperity at all! Quite the opposite, I think! I wonder if Busterites revere fiscal austerity? I hadn't gotten that from the rest of the text."

Catt read the line that Lemmy was indicating. "I don't think it is about austerity, I think it means making the most of nothing. A single penny is worth so little that stopping to pick one up is an act of faith. It doesn't have value, but it could be a symbol of optimism."

"Good, good! I'm glad you saw that, Catt. I'm going to have to revise part of my homily for the ceremony. Would you mind taking care of the morning appointments for me?"

"I would be happy to," said Catt.

Over the remainder of the morning, Catt prayed for safety with a group of travellers, recited a blessing on a portable shrine to a Vulture god, and performed a devotion for the health of Ms Smink, a temple regular who was suffering from a bad cough.

After the devotion was complete, Catt insisted, "Ms Smink, you should go down the street to the apothecary and get a Potion of Soothing for the cough."

"No, no, divinity will suffice," Ms Smink said, waving her hand dismissively.

"You should get a potion," Catt persisted, "Zigmondsnacker is a pragmatic god, medicine will make it easier for him to bless you."

Ms Smink gingerly replaced the faded red hat she had removed before the devotion. "Yes, but no, no, I don't think I need–" Ms Smink was unable to finish the sentence because of a fit of coughing into her handkerchief that doubled her over and dislodged the hat.

Catt picked up the hat and handed it back to Ms Smink.

"Besides," said Ms Smink, "everything at the apothecary is so expensive."

"That's no excuse," Catt said firmly. She walked over to the offering box on the wall beside the main altar, lifted the lid, and fished around for a Shmoud among all the Thorbs.

"Oh, no, no! I couldn't!" protested Ms Smink as Catt tried to press the silver coin into her hand.

"Did the Avatar of Zigmondsnacker refuse the morsel of the Sage's Liver when it was offered?" Catt asked.

Ms Smink suppressed another cough before admitting, "Yes, no, yes, he did take it, he did!"

"Then you take this," Catt instructed. She succeeded this time in placing the coin in the woman's hand. "Buy a potion, get some rest. We'll be counting on your voice at next week's Wailing And Chanting."

Ms Smink capitulated, and taking her hat and the Shmoud, left the temple in a cloud of thanks and coughs.

Catt noticed that Lemmy had left off his notes and was watching her.

"I'm sorry about that," Catt apologized. "You can take that one out of my pay."

"Nonsense! I would have done the same thing. I'm proud of you!" Lemmy said. He was toothily smiling from ear to ear.

Catt shrugged and smiled back. "It seemed right."

"You're not just an excellent acolyte," Lemmy continued, "You're on a fine trajectory to become the second Polypantheonic Priest– if that aligns with your ambitions, that is."

Catt felt her face flush at the flattery. "I'll have to think about that, but thank you," she said.

## Moon

High Priest Lemmy walked up the steep winding switchbacks that led up to the highest hill in the Temple Hill district. This was the eponymous "Hill" that the district was named for. The foundations of the old temple still stood, supporting the newer architecture of the Immutable Library which rose above them.

Lemmy's legs ached with exhaustion, and he was silently saying prayers to Rotosk, god of a thousand spinal columns to stave off the same pain in his back. He had already been tired after officiating the Busterite wedding ceremony, but this was the last appointment of a busy day, and then he could go home and rest.

If Catt was tired, she didn't show it. She was walking slowly, letting him set the pace. Lemmy appreciated that she had not suggested carrying him. It would have been more convenient for both of them, but it would have also felt undignified. As a very small person, Lemmy highly valued his independence, and he felt as if Catt understood and respected that, even though they had never discussed it. In their work together at the temple, Catt did all the heavy lifting, but she was never patronizing about it.

"It doesn't look welcoming," Catt commented, looking up at the Immutable Library's sheer edifice, illuminated by the red light of the setting sun.

"It was a fortress before it was a library," Lemmy said. "It is about six hundred and fifty years old... that part is anyway, these parts here," Lemmy indicated the deeply weathered curved slabs that the switchback road cut through, "these could be thousands of years old."

Catt whistled.

After a few more turns they reached the door, a small modern thing cut neatly into the center of the much larger rust-iron portcullis.

Walking through the door was like walking into a different world. Outside was ancient stone and long shadows, but inside was bright and warm, contemporary in decor, and smelling faintly of cinnamon and tea leaves.

Lemmy had been here before, but this was Catt's first time. He observed her eyes as they flit back and forth, drinking in the atmosphere of the place.

The spacious lobby of the Immutable Library was filled with students, young and old, sitting at tables and benches, sipping at drinks, reading quietly, or having conversations in hushed voices.

The arches of the high ceiling were decorated with vibrant murals, and there were touches of green from illusions of exotic plants and trees scattered around the room.

They moved through the lobby to the stairwell, and Lemmy checked in at the reception desk. "Good evening! We are here to see Professor Memnestralux."

"High Priest Lemmy?" the receptionist confirmed. "Yes, you are on the list, I'll have someone show you up."

A library attendant ushered them into a tiny elevator.

"How does this work?" Catt asked excitedly as the small booth rose upwards, "Is it lifting us with magic?"

"Not exactly," said the attendant, "There's a system of pulleys and counterweights to minimize the work, and a sand treadle at the top that provides the locomotive force and that has to be reloaded daily by students from the athletics department. The actuation and control signals are the only magical part."

"That must be these here," speculated Catt, examining the panel of Arashan runes.

"Please don't touch those," reproved the attendant.

From the top of the elevator, there was one additional flight of stairs, leading to the wide flat open rooftop of the Immutable Library.

"You'll find her at that corner," the attendant indicated. "Touch this 'call' rune when you are ready to go back down.

Lemmy could see the sky and the mountains, and nothing else of the city. There was a low parapet all around the rooftop, but Lemmy could not see over it.

Near the corner of the roof furthest away from the mountains, there was a pair of small shacks perched perilously on the edge, with an array of apparatus between them. Lemmy knew these would be the telescopes.

There were no magical lanterns anywhere on the roof, and this corner seemed somehow even darker.

"Hello!" said Catt.

"Greetings," replied a mellow voice from somewhere.

Lemmy still couldn't see the professor. Catt's eyes must have adjusted to the dark more quickly than his own.

"Professor Memnestralux I presume?" Lemmy said into the black night air.

"You presume correctly," said the voice, "You must be the priest of the Polypantheonic Temple. You come highly recommended by one of my favorite students."

Focusing on the voice, Lemmy was finally able to make out the outline of the speaker, among the silhouettes of the telescopes. She was big, bigger than Catt.

"How may we help you, Professor?" Lemmy asked. The letter inviting him to the Library roof had been cordial but vague. Lemmy had not really known how to prepare himself for the meeting with the illustrious Professor, which had been part of the reason he had asked Catt to accompany him.

"I need your help finding a special god," said the Professor, "Come closer, there are seats here."

Lemmy approached. The telescopes loomed overhead. He was glad to have a place to sit. He sighed audibly as he took his weight off his tired feet.

Catt didn't sit. She went right up to the parapet and leaned over it, and seemed to be surveying the view of the city.

"This is my acolyte and apprentice, Catt Zago," Lemmy said, gesturing at Catt's back.

Catt looked over her shoulder, "It is a pleasure to meet you, Professor Memnestralux." said Catt politely.

"Likewise," said the Professor. "Please call me Memne. I only make students say all those syllables."

Lemmy could see the Professor better now that he was closer. She was sitting close by, facing him. Her shape was complicated by the feathery bulk of her wings. They seemed to be folded back and down, but they still took up a substantial amount of space. Most of her face was difficult to make out, but her eyes shone in the moonlight, with big silvery dilated irises.

"So, Memne, if I may, you say you are looking for a god? Which god? Or which sort of god?" Lemmy felt pleased to be asking. Now that he knew what the meeting was about, he was anticipating a pleasant discussion.

"I'm seeking a god who can assist me with my work."

"So then you are looking for a moon god?" queried Lemmy, "Your student Octinny tells me that you teach Lunarmancy."

"No," answered Memne firmly, "not a moon god. I've exhausted the limits of the tools of my craft, and I need more precision to complete my current project. I've prayed to moon gods, and they've all been utterly useless."

Lemmy didn't like to hear a whole category of deities categorized as useless. "Perhaps we just need to find the *right* moon god," he suggested.

"No," Memne refused, "they are all full of stories about the moon, rationalizations of its origin, parables of its purpose– in short, moon gods only care about how the moon relates to people."

Lemmy was taken aback. Relating the divine to people seemed to him like a nice succinct summary of why gods were so important.

"*I don't care about moon gods*," insisted Memne. "What I care about is the moon itself. The floating ball of rock."

"Rock?" queried Lemmy. He noticed that Catt had turned her back on the city, and was now watching them and listening.

"Have you ever looked at the moon?" was the Professor's reply.

Lemmy kept his mouth shut. He wasn't sure how to interpret this question.

Fortunately, Memne made herself clear.

"Come," she said, "look at it now," she unfolded a wing and stretched it towards the nearest telescope, "This one is designed to track the moon's path."

Lemmy was curious. He got up and made his way over to the base of the telescope. Memne moved also, carefully it seemed, as if she was making an effort to keep her wings back so they would not obstruct him.

In the dimness, Lemmy could make out the eyepiece of the telescope. Memne extended her clawed hand, and began adjusting a knob. Seeing her claws clearly for the first time, Lemmy could see that her talons were capped with curved sheaths of what looked like corkwood.

"This was calibrated for my eye," she explained, as she spun the knob.

Lemmy looked through the eyepiece. He saw bright blurry light, which felt surprising in contrast to the dark night.

"You can adjust it further as you need," suggested Memne.

Lemmy took hold of the knob and turned it slowly. Suddenly a spectacular landscape jumped into focus.

"My goodness!" exclaimed Lemmy. It was not a landscape, but the moonscape, filling the whole of his vision. The faint blotches and discolorations he was familiar with becoming mighty ring-shaped mountain ranges, and vast silvery seas.

"Beautiful, yes?" said Memne.

Lemmy barely nodded, not yet wanting to remove his eye from the eyepiece.

"But the beauty of the moon is not what I am most interested in," Memne asserted, "what I am most interested in is the movement of the moon."

"The movement?" Lemmy asked.

"Yes... how much do you know, High Priest, about the way the moon moves?"

Lemmy finally took his eye away from the telescope. "Yes, yes... well, I do know some."

"May I?" asked Catt.

Lemmy moved aside so that Catt could take a turn looking at the moon.

"I know that the moon moves in a circle in the sky, and that its angle is always predictable, but varies slightly depending upon where in the world one views it from."

"Precisely," confirmed Memne. "The so-called Lunar Gyre Variation."

Catt hummed in admiration of the view through the eyepiece.

Lemmy continued, "And I know that measurements of that variance are said to permit one to calculate the location of the Center Of The World, and that the kingdom of Arash is generally agreed to be at that center."

"More precise calculations put it in the desert north-west of Arash proper," corrected Memne. "Anything else?"

Lemmy thought, trying to think of anything else relevant to the movement of the moon, while excluding the more fanciful stories, like those of a divine dung-beetle pushing the moon through the sky.

Catt lifted her head, and interjected, "I remember a story about a distant land that was so far from the center of the world that the moon would pass directly overhead once each month, and that the people tried to build a tower all the way up to it."

"Good, yes," said Memne. "That is the legend of Lulkismar. It is apocryphal of course, but I have corresponded directly with Lunarmancers who have travelled far enough to take measurements, and establish that *is* plausible– the idea of being able to travel to the edge of the sun-lit world and be directly beneath the path of the moon– not the part about the tower. The tower strikes me as whimsy."

"Is this what your studies are about?" asked Lemmy. "Measuring the moon's movements to discover the center and the edges of the world?"

Catt returned to the eye-piece.

"That is a fine field of study, but no," said Memne. She shifted back to where she had been sitting before.

Lemmy followed, and retook his seat.

Memne's eyes glanced, gleaming, towards the sky, and then focused back on Lemmy again. "I am interested in a *different* aspect of the moon's movements... Tell me, how long does it take the moon to complete a single gyre of the sky?"

"A month. Twenty-eight days."

Memne was silent.

"Close to twenty-eight days," Lemmy corrected himself. "I believe it is just a little bit longer than that, which is why the position of the moon changes slightly on the same day of each year."

"But the size of that *just a little bit*, that is what I am interested in," said Memne. "It is called the Lunar Surplus Ratio, and it is very close to one twenty-eighth of a day."

Lemmy nodded, although he did not understand yet.

"Very close to one twenty-eighth of a day," continued Memne, "but not exactly... it is longer than that by very close to one twenty-eighth of a twenty-eighth."

"Very close to?" asked Lemmy, guessing where this would go next.

"Yes, the Second Degree Surplus Ratio, is larger by very close to one twenty-eighth of one twenty-eighth of one twenty-eighth."

"I see, I see, and this pattern goes on forever, to ever smaller fractions of a day," said Lemmy.

"Forever is what everyone assumes!" said Memne, as if she was exasperated that Lemmy had jumped to that obvious conclusion.

Catt had left the telescope, and now sat herself down near Lemmy and listened.

Memne continued, "Very long ago, Lunarmancers succeeded in measuring the Surplus Ratio down to the Fifth Degree, and the pattern holds, each irregularity was confirmed to be one twenty-eighth smaller than the irregularity before, and the infinitely recursive nature of the Surplus Ratio was taken for granted." Memne seemed to be growing more excited as she spoke. "I have refined the methods of calculating, and have confirmed the Sixth Degree Surplus Ratio holds as well... but the seventh? Well, by the time you get down to the seventh degree, the amount of time we are talking about is incredibly small!"

"Like a blink of an eye?" Lemmy suggested.

Memne laughed, "Oh ho ho! Even the Fourth Degree is faster than the blink of an eye, so the Seventh is so tiny it is difficult to even imagine it without the proper mathematical perspective."

"How could anyone ever measure an amount of time so small?" Catt spoke up.

"On the scale of the movement of the Moon in a single night, no, you can't," Memne vouched, "but suppose you scale up to a year? That is one hundred and forty days. Suppose you measure the moon's movements over ten years? That's one thousand four hundred days. To measure the Lunar Surplus Ratio precisely it is necessary to measure the moon's position over many many days."

Catt had a confused look on her face. She was tapping the fingers of her hand as if counting something.

"How does a god fit into all this?" asked Lemmy.

"I think that my studies might already constitute an act of worship towards a god of precise measurements," said Memne. "I want to learn the name and identity of any such god, so that I can properly beseech them for help in refining the accuracy of–"

"Wait a moment," Catt interrupted. "Did you just say one hundred and forty days in a year?"

"Yes. Twenty-eight days in a month, five months in a year," said Memne in a tone that was a little scornful, and that betrayed annoyance at being interrupted.

"There are twelve months in a year!" Catt exclaimed.

Lemmy looked at Catt, wondering why she was so confused. Why would she think there were so many months?

"Are you talking about the Arashan calendar?" Memne asked. "Are you from there?"

"Arash, and Srappa, and Jen, and everywhere!" Catt protested. "There's only one calendar!"

"Hardly," said Memne, her initial annoyance softening, and taking on a tone of pity. "We use the Shoming calendar in Great Bakak. It has five months."

"I've heard of a long calendar used in some places, but I didn't realize it was so widespread," said Lemmy, placatingly.

"May we continue?" asked Professor Memne.

Catt nodded. She looked stricken, and Lemmy wondered why she would be so embarrassed about a simple cultural misunderstanding. Normally she would have taken such a small blunder in stride.

"As I was saying," Memne resumed, "a god of precise measurements could help me to improve the accuracy of my observations and the accuracy of my timekeeping, and it might be possible for me to prove or disprove the consistency of the Seventh Degree Lunar Surplus Ratio on a scale that fits within the span of my own lifetime."

"Excuse me..." mumbled Catt, and she was up and gone, moving away across the dark roof.

Lemmy looked after her, puzzled, but then turned back to Memne. "I'm certain that with a little research, I can find the deity that you are looking for. I already have a few ideas..."

## Shorter

Catt was back in the elevator. The attendant looked at her, as if expecting more conversation, but Catt's mind was elsewhere, counting days. Two months? She wasn't certain, but she thought that was how long she had been living in Great Bakak. How had she not realized there were only five months in a year?

Catt passed through the library lobby. The brightness seemed a blur now. The air smelled cloying. A sense of urgency had gripped her. She had only three months left, not the ten months she had imagined. Ten felt like forever. Three felt like nothing.

Outside the night was cool and still. Catt ran down the winding switchbacks, and through the streets of Temple Hill. How could she have ever thought of going back to her little narrow lonely bed? What did the show of independence prove? And to whom?

# Note Taking

Segna had come to the conclusion that she could not afford to put her faith in the Seneschal of Delays. The Seneschal had encyclopedic knowledge of the implementation delays that would be imposed on every possible royal decree she could make, but she could not trust the Seneschal to keep track of what she had actually decreed or when each delayed decree was to go into effect. Those things she would have to keep track of herself if she wanted to have any hope of checking and verifying that a decree had actually happened in a timely manner.

Furthermore, many decrees were dependent on each other. A decree to create a royal office tasked with looking after the welfare of orphaned children had a six week delay on it, but that could not even be started until the completion of the two week delay in allocating funds from the royal treasury, which could be slowed further by the high court if she failed to wait for the additional two week delays to implement her proposed changes to guild and league taxation laws which would enable her to sustain the funding.

Segna was sitting curled up in her big chair by the wide balcony, trying to take notes.

Segna had found a large blank scholar's journal amongst her boxes of old things, and had dedicated it to a careful accounting of each decree she had made, and a calendar of when subsequent decrees could be safely made for optimal efficiency. If she relied on her advisors to remind her about such things, she was likely to waste precious days, or worse, forget things entirely.

Segna searched her memory, trying to remember all of her recent meetings, and consultations. She had been getting better at this with practice, but it was harder this evening because she was trying to remember two days instead of one. This was always the case on the day after one of Catt's visits. The night before they had dined together, talked privately for hours in the royal bathhouse, and slept entwined through the night.

She had not touched the journal. She had not even let Catt know that the journal existed. Now she was exerting her recollection, trying to summon back the details of conversations she had made with city dignitaries a day and a half ago.

A loud knock sounded on the door to her quarters.

"I'm busy! Come back in the morning," Segna called out, trying to put a little extra regal force into her voice. She didn't want to be bothered by the servants right now, and in the unlikely event that it was an advisor with an emergency, they could shout through the door if it was so important.

The knock did not repeat. There was no voice. Segna settled back to her journal. She wrote a few more lines of notes.

Catt flopped over the corner of the balcony as if she had just clambered out of thin air.

# Argument

"Catt!" Segna exclaimed, jumping up, "how did you–?"

"Your walls are incredibly easy to climb," Catt said, dusting herself off.

Segna came close to Catt and looked over the balcony. It was a long way down. She looked sideways and saw a perilously narrow ledge.

Catt took ahold of Segna's hands. "I don't want you to die!" she said.

"What are you talking about? Was that you at the door? Why didn't you say anything?" Segna asked, still surprised and confused.

"I can't let them kill you!" Catt whispered to her, "I want to save you somehow!"

"Oh, no, no, Catt, what are you saying?" asked Segna, although she suddenly understood very clearly exactly what Catt was talking about, and didn't wait for an answer, "Why now? Where is this coming from? You weren't like this last night."

Catt looked at her sheepishly, "I just realized how short a year is. I don't want to be without you."

Segna embraced Catt, "Put it out of your mind," she said. "I just want to enjoy the time that we have while we have it."

Catt gently pushed her back a little bit, "No! I want more! It's not enough! I want more of you. There has to be a way of getting out of this."

Segna felt dread welling up within her. This was the topic that she had not allowed herself to think about– *could not* allow herself to think about, and here was Catt dredging it to the surface.

"I can't," Segna protested, "dying is just part of being King."

"Let's run away!" Catt said, squeezing Segna's arms. "We can get some horses and just go!"

Segna closed her eyes and took a deep breath. "The Executioners Guild doesn't allow Kings to quit. They would ride us down on the road."

"Then we stay off the road!"

"And die of thirst in the desert?" asked Segna. "Is that what you want Catt? To die of thirst in the desert with me?"

"No!" said Catt, "I want to live! I want *us* to live!"

Segna took Catt's hand and walked back to the chair. She picked up the journal from where it had fallen on the floor, and placed it on the little table.

Segna sat on the edge of the chair. Catt stood and looked down at her.

"What I want," Segna said earnestly, "Is for you to help me feel happiness while I still can, and after I'm... gone, I want you to go on living. Knowing you will still be there makes this easier for me."

"But what if there is a way to escape?" Catt persisted. "Forget the desert, there has to be another way. What if we disguise ourselves and join a caravan?"

"That won't work," Segna felt angry at Catt for forcing her to break it down. "It hasn't happened in almost two hundred years, but faithless Kings are hunted down. There are stories about it. It used to happen more often in olden times."

"So you're saying they are out of practice?" said Catt with a grin.

"Stop it, I'm serious," Segna scolded, "If you don't believe me, ask the Prime Archivist, they have records that go back– No, you know what? Forget I said that. Don't talk to anyone about this. I don't want anyone knowing that you've been thinking about this!"

"Okay," said Catt, "I'll keep quiet, and we'll come up with a plan together."

"No, Catt!" Segna said forcefully. She felt frustrated. "It isn't possible, and fixating on the impossible will just ruin what time we have left."

"Why is it impossible?" demanded Catt.

"You'll get yourself in trouble!" Segna said, "the penalty for aiding a faithless King is death, and not a painless one!"

"Doesn't that make you mad?" asked Catt, "that they're going to kill you and anyone who tries to help you?"

"You're making me mad!" Segna cried. "You're being selfish!"

Catt was looking at Segna with furrowed brow. She looked confused. How could Catt not be getting this?

"I'm selfish?" asked Catt, "because I want to risk my life to save your life?"

Segna put her face in her hands. "Catt, why Can't you let *me* be selfish? I thought I had found someone who was going to love me for the rest of my life, for whatever that's worth. Now if you drive us apart because you can't accept reality, then I won't even get to have that much!"

Catt didn't say anything.

"I would rather we end it now," said Segna, "so I can know you're still alive somewhere, rather than for you to make a stupid sacrifice that won't change what happens to me."

Segna felt tears between her fingers. Catt was still saying nothing.

With her face covered, Segna imagined Catt slipping away, climbing back over the balcony, and disappearing. Segna uncovered her face and looked up, ready to shout *"No, use the door!"*.

Catt was still there, crouching right in front of her. Her face was close enough to touch.

"I hear you," said Catt. "I'm not going to leave you."

Segna hiccuped.

"I'm not going to stop wishing for a miracle," Catt continued, "but I won't let it come between us, and I won't do anything stupid. I promise."

"What good is a promise like that from a woman who climbs sheer walls instead of going through the door?" Segna said, sobbing and laughing at the same time. She grabbed Catt and pulled her closer.

Catt sat beside Segna, and held her.

# Tattoo

Catt woke from a dream. She had been on the deck of a ship, pitching in the waves, but instead of the pirates she remembered from her childhood, the deck had been full of people from Great Bakak. The captain had been shouting that a storm was coming, and Catt had been seized by the terror of knowing what was coming, while the others had been dancing and celebrating the promise of rain. *"A storm! A storm!"* the captain had bellowed menacingly. *"A storm! A storm!"* Lemmy had sung joyously.

The wind had raged, the black clouds had opened up, but instead of rain, fire had fallen from the sky instead.

Now she was awake.

She was in the middle of the big round bed. Segna was close by, snoring softly, half covered by the sheets.

Catt sat up and moved a little closer. She looked down at Segna's face, and watched her breathe. Softly, trying not to wake her, Catt put her hand on Segna's belly.

Segna stirred a little, but did not wake. Her hand moved and touched Catt's.

Catt looked at the tattoos on Segna's skin. She knew it was a magical spell. She had been unable to read it the first time she saw it, but now having looked at Segna's beginner's book of magic, Catt found that she actually could make out some of the words, Arashan vocabulary in the Shoming alphabet, artistically stylized.

**"To go suddenly"**

**"Awayness"**

**"Only what makes me myself"**

**"Exactly where I put my mind"**

**"Escaping abyss"**

There were many words that Catt didn't know, and things that she recognized as what Segna had described as variables, and the whole thing was laced together with the lines of a focus diagram, more complex than any Catt had seen in the pages of the book.

Catt re-read the words she understood. She didn't know what the spell did, but the words filled her with determination. It felt like she was reading a prayer, one that was pleading for the very same hope she had already set her heart on, and it was written there in silvery beauty on the skin of her sleeping lover.

# Faithless

Catt had been back to the Immutable Library already. She had found the floors where the non-magical books were kept, and had located the shelves devoted to local histories.

She had found a fair number of books about the history of Great Bakak's kings, but they had all been dry essays, lists of royal statistics, and a few biographies of some of the more noteworthy kings.

What she had failed to find was any details about the "faithless" kings. They were nothing more than footnotes and appendices, making it clear that those kings who tried to shirk their royal duty to die had been punished, killed without honor. Their decrees had been cancelled, their deeds had been forgotten. There were no useful details about them to be found in the library.

While pondering this failure later, Catt remembered that Segna had said that there were "stories" about the faithless kings. What if they were the wrong sort of stories to find in a reputable library?

Catt walked to her apartment. She had not slept there even once in the week since she had decided to steal the King, but it was still hers. She was still paying for it. She would stop by occasionally to check on her seed sprouts and to have tea with Ms Bethen.

"Good afternoon, Dearie!" The landlady called. She was sitting on the front steps. Beside her was one of the children who lived in the building. They seemed to be playing some kind of game with a bunch of polished rocks arrayed on a carved board.

"Hello, Ms Bethen, hello Disty," Catt greeted them.

"We've missed you lately!" said Ms Bethen.

Disty smiled at Catt, and then went on poking thoughtfully at the stones, as if counting.

"I have a theatre question," Catt began. "Are you familiar with a play about a King who tries to run away from the Executioners?"

Ms Bethen frowned and shook her head. "No, I've not heard of that one," she said. "It sounds like it would be in poor taste. Why do you ask."

"Oh, someone at the temple told me about it," Catt lied, "but they had seen it so long ago, they couldn't remember how it ended."

"Only one way that could end," Ms Bethen tutted.

Disty was looking up. "I know that one!" the child said excitedly, I know someone at school who has a book about it! They catch the bad king in the desert and chop him up! Not just the neck, but all into little pieces, starting from the toes and up to the top. It has woodcut illustrations and everything. Then they do the same to all the servants that he took with him to carry the treasure he stole."

Ms Bethen stared at Disty disapprovingly. "I don't mind a good tragedy now and then, but that sounds quite disgusting!"

Disty shrugged. "It wasn't my book, it was Bilarg's. I just got to see it. It had lots of gross pictures. Teacher said not to bring it anymore."

"I should hope not," said Ms Bethen. "Now, are you going to make a move or not?"

Disty picked up four rocks and redistributed them around the board.

"Catt, would you like to play the winner?" asked Ms Bethen, as she pondered the board.

"Thank you, but I can't," said Catt. "I just came to change and then I'm off again."

"Dinner with your mysterious girlfriend again?" pried Ms Bethen.

Catt blushed in spite of herself.

"When are you going to bring her by and introduce her, Dearie?" asked Ms Bethen.

Catt stepped over the gameboard and moved up the steps. "Someday, I hope," she said.

# Woodcuts

*Pulp Scribe* was a small shop wedged between a fashionable bar and a tattoo parlor in the east end of Marketday.

The shelves were packed with periodicals, pamphlets, and thin cheaply bound books. Almost everything seemed to be printed on the same cheap paper stock, and the whole place smelled of ink. From the back room came the continuous tapping of several chisels, and the occasional clack and groan of a movable type press, but the front of the shop was otherwise quiet.

No other customers were present as Catt browsed the shelves. The clerk behind the counter stared at her. They had very old and tired eyes looking out of an otherwise young seeming face. Their eyes were heavily accented with thick dark blue makeup which might have hidden some wrinkles but did nothing to conceal an air of weariness.

Catt tried to ignore the clerk, and just focused on the books.

"**Monsters and Daemons of the Desert**"
"**Beasts Who Drink Blood**"
"**Most Notorious Murderers**"
"**Easy Curses For Your Enemies**"
And there it was;
"**Chilling Tales of Faithless Kings**"

Catt picked it up. It was a thin volume. The cover was just a heavier paper, it was not even properly bound.

She flipped through it. There were woodcut illustrations on every other page. The type was cramped and the margins narrow. She almost immediately stumbled upon the illustrations that Disty had mentioned of a person being chopped up feet first. The executioners were almost up to the chest. There was a crowd of other people in the background, tied up awaiting their fate, with half a dozen other axe-wielders standing guard.

Catt read some of the text on the facing page.

*"...into the deep and trackless desert whereupon the faithless and entourage set up camp by a small Oasis and proceeded to build dwellings of stone and clay. Trackers of The Guild spotted them on the two thousand nine hundred and twenty seventh day, and reinforcements arrived three weeks later. The Guild encircled the camp of the faithless, and fell upon them in the night, and..."*

Catt's mouth felt dry. Two thousand nine hundred and twenty seven days? That was a serious search. The Executioners would not give up easily.

Catt went to the counter. "I'll take this," she said, getting her coins.

"Two Thorbs," the clerk said, and then squinting at the book they added, "Heh. If this is what you're into, you should check the side room." They jerked a thumb towards a black-curtained partition. "We keep the explicit stuff over there."

Catt shook her head. "Maybe another time," she deflected. She gave over the two coins.

"You want a bag for that?" the clerk asked. There was a stack of frayed brown paper sacks on the corner of the desk.

"Sure," Catt agreed amiably, accepting one.

As Catt tucked her purchase into the bag, the clerk leaned out over the counter, as if trying to look past her out the door.

In a lower voice, the clerk whispered, "Hey! You look like someone who might like Reff. You need some Reff?"

"Not really?" she answered, unsure what "Reff" might be.

"No? That's a shame. I got some extra. Cheap."

"Thanks, but not really my thing." Catt edged a step closer to the door.

"What is your thing?" asked the clerk. "We might have it. Polymorph? Forget-me-yes? Shira's Sleep?"

"I'll remember that if I want any later, Thanks!" said Catt quickly, and she left before the conversation could continue.

# Wand

The stories were pretty grim.

Catt sat near the window of her little apartment intending to read through the whole dreadful thing. She didn't dare take it with her where Segna might see it. It would be upsetting to her.

Catt had to be honest with herself. She was upset by it too. The tales were exaggerated and quite possibly they were just the product of the author's vivid imagination, but in a few ways they were very consistent. The executioners were ruthless and persistent, and the faithless king always met a horrible end.

Several kings had made escapes, either alone or with accomplices, but they were always hunted down, even at great distances. One made it all the way to Arash before being caught and cut down. Another was caught on the shores of the green sea, trying to stow away in a fishing boat.

One king hired a troop of barbarian mercenaries to defend her and fight the executioners at the Regicide ceremony. She died in the fight, but that didn't stop the executioners from slaying every last barbarian, and sending a wagon full of their heads all the way back to Odok as a warning.

Another king had walled themselves up in a wine cellar in the catacombs under the palace. It had taken the executioners twenty six years to discover where that king had vanished to...

Catt did the math to convert the years into the calendar she was more familiar with... about elven years then, less impressive than it had seemed at first.

Nevertheless, they had still decapitated the skeleton, just to drive home the point that a faithless king could not escape their fate.

Catt took a break from the reading and stared out the window for a while. The evening was beautiful. The sinking sun was very red, and the shadows on the buildings were striking.

The window ledge was now fully a shrine. Five sprouting seed pits were growing up from five clay cups full of dirt. One of the sprouts was almost as tall as Catt's hand, and had produced a few tiny bright green leaves. Just inside the window was a tray covered with accumulated scraps from Catt's lunches, in various states of decay. A neat and orderly trail of ants led from the window to the tray and back out again. They did not stray elsewhere in the room. The smell was pungent and earthy, but surprisingly not at all unpleasant. The upper part of the window had been filled by a pair of almost perfectly symmetrical spider webs.

"I know you don't give luck," Catt said to Hret-ret-akl, "but I could use some anyway. I need to find a way to save my love, and it has to be a better plan than; *Run away and hope these stories are fabricated*"

Hret-ret-akl didn't answer. Catt didn't really expect her to. Maybe a more talkative god would have sent the spiders to spell out an omen across the webs, but it seemed that Hret-ret-akl was not that kind of goddess. Or she was not listening. Or she was too far away. Or she was too weak here, so very far away from anything like a forest.

Catt returned to her chair and continued studying the book.

Some of the kings tried to use magic. One king paid a wizard to cast a potent illusion to animate a fresh corpse and make it appear to be the king. The executioners beheaded the apparition, but they had a powerful magic wand that could detect and lay bare any spell, so the ruse was quickly discovered. The faithless king was found and killed before they could get a day's journey away, and the wizard met the same end.

Catt remembered the wand. She had been preoccupied by emotion and surprise, but she remembered seeing it.

The book claimed that the wand had always been a tool at the disposal of the Guild of Executioners, but that after that particular incident, they had made it into a formal part of the Regicide ceremony.

Catt pushed her chair back, balancing it on two legs while she put her feet up on the table.

Maybe there was something to the wand. Some of the other tales mentioned it too. The executioners seemed to rely on it to thwart any faithless king who tried to use magic to aid their escape. What if there was a way to deceive or neutralize the wand? Maybe that would open up new opportunities. Maybe it would be possible to cast a spell to fool them into thinking Segna was dead when she wasn't.

# Best Drinks

"So, tell me, where are the best places to drink in Great Bakak?"

The parishioner's bloodshot eyes lit up. "Oh ho ho! There are so many!" he said, barely slurring his words. He was a devout of The Merry Twins, and Catt was walking him home after a fete of fermented drink at the Polypantheonic Temple.

"Well, what if you had to pick the best?" Catt asked.

"We're going the wrong way," he said, jerking unsteadily against her arm. "The best ones are all back in Temple Hill."

Catt prevented him from changing direction.

"Just tell me about them," she said. "I can't go now. I have to get back and help High Priest Lemmy clean up."

"Okay, okay. Wizards love good booze. Students love too much booze. The bars around there are the place to get too much good booze. *Halfdragon's*? Excellent. *Stick and Stone*? Too crowded, but fantastic. But my favorite... I think it is *The Green Beard*. They brew it all there, and they get creative."

"So that's where you usually go?" Catt asked.

"Nah, no," said the man, "too expensive. And too long a walk... sometimes the best... isn't the best, you know?" He flailed a limp hand in the air to emphasize the point.

They were getting closer to the terraced fields of Granary Hill. He lived in one of the farmhouses there. Catt double checked the paper that Lemmy had written the address on.

"Now local," the man continued, "one of my favorites is The Farmer's Guild Clubhouse. They do amazing things with malts and flashgrass root, I'm not a member anymore, but they have open house nights almost every week."

Catt saw the opportunity to steer the conversation in the direction she wanted. "So that's where the Farmer's Guild members all drink? Do all the guilds have places like that?" she asked.

"Mmm... lots of them, yeah, I guess. Climbers Guild is supposed to have a club up in the rocks you can only get to with ropes. I've never been. Not as young as I used to be."

"What about the Executioner's Guild? Where do they drink?"

The man chuckled, "Oh, there's a place called The Hidden Smile up on brickstack road that caters to 'em. It's terrible. The drinks are so weak, might as well be water. They ain't supposed to get drunk on the job. I think if one of them wants a proper drink, they have to wait until their shift is over, and take the mask and cape off."

# Hidden Smile

You didn't have to be an executioner to drink at the Hidden Smile, but you did have to wear a mask.

Catt was wearing a red felt mask stiffened with wires that she had found at a shop earlier that week. She sat at a table in the corner of the Hidden Smile, picking at her dinner and sipping at her drink. All the food served here was cut into small pieces to be easy to slip under a mask or through a mouth-hole. All the drinks were served with long waxed-paper straws for the same reason. In spite of that accommodation, many of the customers were wearing half-masks that only covered their eyes and noses. Catt got the impression that this was considered fashionable in some circles.

There had only been a handful of actual executioners here each of the three consecutive nights that Catt had dined here before going to see Segna.

A good opportunity to chat with one of them had not presented itself. They tended to come in small groups or pairs, and sit with their axes leaning against their tables, speaking to one another in low voices, and generally giving the impression that they were patronizing this mask-friendly bar only grudgingly.

Tonight however, Catt spotted the chance she had been looking for.

A party of three executioners had finished their meal. Two of them had paid and left, but the third one had remained at the table and ordered a second drink.

Catt waited until the drink was half empty, and then abandoned her own table and approached the lone executioner.

"Mind if I sit?" Catt asked.

The wooden mask looked up as if surprised, but then nodded. "Sure, go ahead."

The executioner was slight of build, and sounded young.

Catt sat, and flagged down a passing server. "Two more, please!"

Catt nodded towards the axe. "How many people have you killed with that?" she asked conversationally.

The executioner laughed. She really did sound young. Catt guessed she couldn't be more than twenty... Wait, no... fifty? Forty five? Catt was still not comfortable with the Shoming calendar.

"I'm only a Junior," the executioner explained. "You have to be a Senior before you actually get to do an execution."

The server placed two new cups with tall straws on the table. Catt handed over some coin.

"Thanks!" said the executioner. "There really aren't all that many executions anyway. Most of the criminals just get locked up for a while."

"So the axe is just for show?" said Catt, as if she thought it was unfair.

"Well, sort of." said the executioner, "I'm not supposed to chop anyone without a trial, you know?" she drained the remains of her previous drink, and took the one Catt had bought for her.

Catt pretended to sip her own drink.

"I could use it if a criminal pulled a knife on me," said the executioner.

"Oh! That sounds exciting!" said Catt, fighting down a brief wave of nausea.

"But that hasn't happened," admitted the executioner, almost wistfully.

"Still, must be interesting work, catching criminals," Catt suggested.

The executioner shrugged. "When I've got more seniority it will be," she said, "but there are lotteries and waiting lists to get on the rotation for the really good jobs. New juniors have to settle for walking around in the hot sun looking for lawbreaking, or sitting around in the Guild Hall doing paperwork and filing reports for the Seniors."

"Let me guess," said Catt wryly, "you got the hot sun today?"

The executioner chuckled. She had already made a dent in the new drink. "You can tell, huh? Yeah, it was a thirsty day."

"The drinks here aren't the best," said Catt.

"Yeah, they're just so-so, but they're wet."

"You know any better places than this?" asked Catt.

The mask blocked much potential for emotional expression, but the executioner's eyes looked thoughtful.

"There was this great place I used to go," she said.

"Yeah?" Catt prompted.

"It's called *Shortbig House 3*," she said. "Ever heard of it?"

# Shortbig House 3

Catt and the Executioner were walking through the streets of Marketday and the Poor Quarter, and chatting as if they were old friends. Catt had the feeling that her mark really wanted to talk.

As they got deeper into the Poor Quarter, the executioner stopped and said, "I guess my shift is over, and I shouldn't really go in like this," she looked around as if checking to see if anyone other than Catt was watching. Then she reached up and removed her mask.

Catt felt her estimate was confirmed. This Executioner was just barely an adult!

"I'm Junior Executioner Fullbrite, by the way." She offered her hand.

Catt shook it.

"It's nice to make a new friend, Fullbrite," Catt said. "My name is Nora."

"Nora," Executioner Fullbrite repeated. "We're not really supposed to let people know who we are, but you seem cool," she smiled brightly.

"Should I take this off?" Catt said, of the red mask she was still wearing.

Fullbrite shrugged. "Whatever, it's up to you."

"Because I need it to hide my *terrible disfiguring scar!*" Catt said it as if it was a joke.

Fullbrite laughed, but when Catt remained awkwardly silent, Fullbrite said, "Wait... really?"

Now it was Catt's turn to laugh, "No, I'm kidding. I just like it."

"Well it looks good on you," said Fullbrite. "Very fashionable."

And so Catt's face remained hidden.

They continued walking through the Poor Quarter. Catt guessed that they were close to the Caravan Depot, right on the edge of the city. The streets had a lot of blown sand on them, and many of the buildings seemed more dilapidated and less inhabited than most of the rest of the Poor Quarter.

"We're almost there," said Fullbrite, "I want to stash these somewhere. I don't want anyone to know I'm an Axe." She was carrying her mask wrapped up inside her cloak.

Fullbrite slowed and began looking around the darkened street.

"How about there?" Catt suggested, pointing at a half collapsed stairwell in an alleyway.

"Yeah, that'll work, I guess," said Fullbrite, examining the wrecked steps. "I wish I had thought to ditch this stuff at home before we walked all this way."

She peered under the lowest step, and then removing her axe from her belt, she slid it underneath. Then she pushed the wadded cloak and mask after it.

Catt could not believe her good luck. Seeing the opportunity, she said, "I think I'll leave some of my stuff there too." She took out her coin purse from her pocket. "Better not to risk pickpockets," Catt said. She made a show of removing a few Thorbs and dropping them back into her pocket, "For drinks," she explained. The coin purse went under the broken steps as well.

"Good thinking," said Fullbrite, and then looking down at herself, "oh, yeah. This too."

She removed her black shirt with the blue axe over crown emblem, stripping down to just a black singlet and her black trousers. The shirt went under the steps. "This will be better for dancing," she said. "Did I mention there was dancing? There is dancing! It's great!"

Catt surveyed the hiding place. "I can't see anything. Nobody will find that stuff."

They proceeded down the empty sand-blown street. Catt could hear distant music.

"That's it up there," said Fullbrite, pointing down the street. She looked like she was just some youngster on her way to a party. Everything that had made her an executioner had vanished.

Catt saw a row of large tenement buildings, four stories tall each, except for one, which was conspicuously missing, a single story of rubble and blackened brick walls. It was a negative space that drew the eye, like a missing tooth right in the middle of a grin.

"Shortbig House 3 burned down like twenty years ago," said Fullbrite, "we are *way* outside the Unburning here, so that kind of stuff happens sometimes in this part of the City."

Catt nodded. Most of the windows in the nearby buildings were completely dark, making them seem abandoned, but she could see a flickering red light that looked like torchlight coming from the ruined building.

"Some old bard started coming here and holding a vigil for the people who died, and other people came to listen, and it just kind of became a thing,"

"It's a vigil?" Catt asked, surprised. She had been expecting a sketchy bar.

"Sort of, it used to be," said Fullbrite, "now people just come every night and drink and dance and there is always lots of music."

They approached a gap that had been cleared in the rubble, and Catt could see inside Shortbig House 3. The interior was surprisingly clear, as if someone had long ago hauled away all the collapsed remains of the rest of the building. The centerpiece of the space was a big bonfire in the middle. Seeing it felt surreal. Catt had grown so used to the cool steadiness of the magical lanterns in the palace and had become accustomed to doing things by the silvery light of the moon when she was out and about at night, that this big bold bonfire was jarring. It immediately reminded her of the Golem Jangley in the Smokefields, and her promise to write a prayer for them.

All around the bonfire was a loose ring of benches fashioned out of charred beams and stacks of loose bricks. People were sitting, standing, and dancing in the firelight. A pair of musicians were playing, one with a fiddle, and the other with a big plucked string instrument that Catt didn't have a name for.

Up above all this, the firelight and the shadows of the dancers played on the walls of the nearest buildings, presumably Shortbig houses 2 and 4, which had survived that tragic fire that felled their sibling. The whole atmosphere was joyful and welcoming, but also solemn at the same time.

"See?" said Fullbrite, nudging Catt. "I told you it was good!"

"I really like this!" Catt said sincerely, "It's so alive!"

Catt wondered if Lemmy knew about this place, and what he would think about it. She imagined the souls of whoever had died here being comforted by the lasting company of this festive vigil. She knew she was projecting her own feelings, and couldn't guess what the dead really felt, but she also knew it was okay to wish it. This was a different sort of a prayer, that didn't need a specific deity.

# Dance

There was an enterprising person with some kegs of beer on a cart in the corner of the ruins.

Catt bought a couple drinks, and she and Fullbrite sat and listened to the music.

After the fiddler finished, a big lad with dark green skin and a square jaw full of sharp teeth took up position by the fire. He had a pipe flute that he held delicately and played expertly. The small instrument seemed incongruous in contrast to his beefy arms, but he coaxed music out of it so naturally that it seemed to be an extension of himself.

Catt noticed that Fullbrite was staring at the young musician with a thirsty intensity.

"You should ask him to dance after he is done playing!" Catt whispered to her.

Fullbrite giggled and blushed. "No, I couldn't!" she insisted.

After a few minutes, a drummer sitting nearby joined in. The flute player's performance intensified.

"I think he's looking at you," Catt said to Fullbrite.

This was nonsense, the flute player's eyes were clearly closed as he focused on his song, but Fullbrite squirmed all the same, clearly pleased to be complicit in imagining it.

When the flute player finally finished, He sat down and another musician stood up to take his place. His shoulders were heaving and his forehead was shining with sweat. It had been an intense performance, masterfully played.

"Now is your chance!" said Catt, "go ask him!"

"Oh, Nora! I can't! What if he says no?"

"Come on," said Catt, getting up and taking Fullbrite's hand and pulling her along.

"Excuse me!" Catt said to the young man, "My friend wanted to ask you to dance."

He looked up, surprised.

"Um... yes!" squeaked Fullbrite in confirmation.

The flute player shrugged and smiled, "Sure. I'd love to," he stood up.

Catt melted away from the pair as they began to dance. Fullbrite was blushing conspicuously.

As soon as Catt was confident that Fullbrite had forgotten about her, she turned and left Shortbig House 3.

Catt hurried back to the alleyway with the collapsed stairs. She didn't see any other people nearby. Other than the musical vigil, this part of the city seemed either asleep or abandoned.

Catt pulled all the things out of the hiding place. She emptied her coin purse, and wrapped the coins with the mask inside the black shirt and cloak.

Catt then tore the coin purse, and left it on the ground in front of the steps. She carried the black bundle and the axe further down the alleyway until she spotted a heap of garbage and loose sand, almost all the way to the next street. She buried her loot underneath the rubbish, and then hurried back to Shortbig House 3.

She was prepared to claim she had just gone to take a leak, but there was no need for the lie. Fullbrite and the flute player were still dancing, holding each other's arms, eyes locked together.

Catt found a comfortable place on the edge of the firelight to sit and lean back and enjoy the music while she waited.

Catt thought about Segna, and wondered what it would be like to dance with her. They had not had the opportunity yet. Catt didn't even know whether or not Segna liked to dance.

# Theft

"That was the best night ever!" Fullbrite gushed, twirling around as she walked.

"I had fun too," said Catt, honestly, but distractedly. She was anticipating the ensuing discovery.

"He said he wants to see me again. We're going to meet evening after next!"

"It's good that you worked up the courage to talk to him," Catt said, revising history a little.

"I couldn't have done it without you Nora," Fullbrite stooped at the ruined steps. She fished underneath with her hand, "Thank you for... encouraging... me..."

Fullbrite crouched lower, digging under the steps with both hands.

"I can't find... my axe! It has to be..." The pitch of Fullbrite's voice rose in panic.

"What's wrong?" asked Catt.

"I can't find my things!" Fullbrite stood up and looked around frantically, as if there might be a second collapsed stairwell nearby.

"Let me see," Catt said, making a show of getting down on hands and knees to look under the steps.

Fullbrite pounced on the torn coin purse. "Look!" she exclaimed.

Catt was ready for this. "That's my coin purse!" she said, as if surprised, and reached for it.

Fullbrite let her have it.

Catt pulled at the torn edges and peered inside, shaking it to confirm its emptiness.

Fullbrite was walking in tiny circles now. "No, no, no, no!" she mumbled.

Catt went back to reaching under the stairs. "The rest of it has to be here somewhere. Where did all the coins go?"

"Somebody stole it!" Fullbrite wailed. Then she stomped her foot. "Stupid! I can't believe I was so stupid! Why did I leave it here?"

"What? How?" Catt played dumb.

"I should have just walked back home! I can't believe I left it here!"

"What about all my money?" Catt asked, trying to sound equally upset.

"Forget about your money!" Fullbrite snapped angrily. "Do you know how much trouble I'm going to be in? An executioner can't just lose their axe! They can't just lose their mask!"

Catt tried to look shocked, but realized the effect was probably lost because after all this time she was still wearing her own mask. She wondered if Fullbrite was going to demand she take it off. Catt was prepared if suspicion fell on her. She could simply run away, and come back another day to retrieve the things.

But instead, Fullbrite put her face into her hands and sobbed, "What am I going to do, Nora? What am I going to tell the Seniors?"

Catt found herself reaching for Fullbrite's shoulder to comfort her. She felt a twinge of guilt, which she fought hard to ignore.

"I'm going to be in so much trouble. I took an oath to that mask! It can't be gone! They'll probably kick me out of the guild!"

This thought appealed to Catt. The idea of this young woman being expelled from the Guild of Executioners seemed like an ideal outcome. Her guilt was washed away with this rationalization.

Fullbrite might be unhappy now, but losing her job might set her down some other better path instead.

In the end, Catt walked the disconsolate young executioner all the way back to Marketday, to the door that Catt suspected might be Fullbrite's parent's house.

Catt said goodbye to her with some empty words of encouragement, and then when she was alone, she doubled back to fetch the fruits of her theft.

To Catt's annoyance, she kept thinking about whether or not Fullbrite would actually go and meet with the flute player again.

# Foray

Catt's first foray into the Guild Hall of the Executioners was nerve-wracking but uneventful.

The Guild Hall was a large rectangular building at the edge between Old Bakak and Granary Hill. It had no windows, and was built of dull whitish stone. The front doors were wide enough to drive a cart through, and seemed perpetually propped open. On either side of the doors was a flanking pair of stone flowerboxes, filled with a bristle of well-maintained decorative flowering cactuses. The beautiful greens and yellows on either side of the open door made the entrance seem as welcoming as the yawning mouth of a camouflaged ambush predator.

Catt, wearing Fullbrite's uniform, walked right in.

She followed not far behind a real executioner, and pretended that she knew exactly where she was going.

Past the small waiting room full of empty chairs and a handful of civilians sitting in a few of them.

Past the big desk, where the executioner seated there did not so much glance at her.

Past door after door and hallway after branching hallway. Other executioners walked in the halls, or sat at desks behind open doors. Voices sometimes came from behind closed doors.

Nobody paid any special attention to her.

Catt's heart was pounding, but she managed to remain calm, act natural, and move herself forward as if she belonged there.

It felt like an eternity, though really it had only been a few minutes.

With every bit as much confidence and purpose, she turned herself around and headed out the way she had come. She was just an executioner, on her way out into the city to do whatever executioners did.

Her disguise had worked. She now had a rough idea of the layout of the first floor. She had spotted various rooms that might be worthy of further exploration on her next visit. She had proven to herself that she could get away with this intrusion.

There would be more weak points in this organization, and she would find them.

# Routine

There was an envelope on the desk. It was sealed with a small blob of black wax.

Senior Executioner Crocken understood that it was for him, although nothing was written on the exterior of the envelope. The mere fact that it was here on his desk was self-evident proof.

The Reaper often communicated this way. Mask to mask meetings they reserved for only the most important matters.

Crocken leaned his axe against the side of the desk and sat down. His chair creaked comfortably.

He took a letter opener from the desk and slit the envelope.

Inside was a terse handwritten note. It stated that he had been selected once again to wield the Wand of Reveal Magic in the upcoming Regicide festival. There were no words of congratulations, the Reaper would never write anything so sentimental, but their respect for him was implicit, and he could not help but feel a small flicker of pride, which he permitted himself to enjoy for a moment, before setting the letter aside and proceeding with his morning routine.

From a desk drawer he took out his written reports from the previous day, and began to review them. He always finished his reports completely before going home. It was important to record the details of arrests and investigations promptly while the memories were fresh and untainted by dreaming. It was also equally important to check and revise these reports with the emotional distance that only time and rest could bring.

He appended a few small clarifications, and deemed the reports adequate for filing.

He then wrote out his intended schedule for the day. These schedules rarely survived the unpredictable demands of the job, but he found them very useful for keeping himself focused on his professional priorities.

Crocken rose from the chair. Its worn joinery squeaked in familiar parting. He re-fastened his axe on his belt, and took up the stack of reports, and carried them to the records room.

# Filing

The records room was a large meandering irregular space on the second floor. Records only needed to be kept for twelve years before they were destroyed, but the city itself had grown over time, and so also had the record room, with walls being knocked down and adjacent spaces being repurposed.

Crocken added his reports to the piles on the "In" desk. Junior Executioners were moving around the room doing the tedious work of filing things away and updating the cross-indexes.

He was about to leave, when someone called his name.

"Crocken, is that you?"

Crocken stopped and looked back. It was Senior Executioner Ahraft. Ahraft was a short and wide person with a broad mask with small wide-set eye holes. They were the Senior supervisor of the records room.

"Just the person I wanted to speak to," said Ahraft, "Have you time?"

Crocken agreed, and followed Ahraft to a tiny office slightly away from the records room.

Ahraft was holding several loose-leaf binders. They looked down the hall as if expecting to be followed, and then closed the door.

"Look at this!" Ahraft exclaimed, flopping the binders down on the desk.

Crocken was not sure what he was looking at, but Ahraft wasted no time in explaining.

"Look at this mess!" Ahraft flipped through the relatively neat looking pages. "All of these! All of these reports mis-filed!"

Crocken waited patiently.

"Haphazardly stashed all throughout the files, they're all recent files too, from the past two weeks, but someone has been wedging them into random drawers all throughout the historical sections. And these are just the ones I have found so far! And these!" Ahraft grabbed one of the other binders, "This entire stack was wadded in the back of the ZZZ section!"

Crocken took the topmost report and glanced over it. "This isn't a Zed," he said, "suspect name is right here at the top."

"Exactly!" huffed Ahraft, exasperated.

"So are any of these mine?" asked Crocken, beginning to flip through the papers.

"I don't know, I don't care!" said Ahraft. "What I care about is finding which worthless Junior is doing it, and who was responsible for their training, and have both their masks!"

Crocken now understood why this was relevant to himself. Crocken was one of the Senior Executioners responsible for training and orientation of new Juniors.

"If it's one of mine doing it, I will set them straight." Crocken said firmly.

"If it's one of yours I would hope you flay them!" Ahraft said.

"Did you say these were all recent?" asked Crocken. He flipped through a few more, checking the dates.

"From two weeks ago, to two days ago," said Ahraft. "That's all I've found so far, but it's going to take me forever to check all the active drawers."

"I'll see if I can find any Intermediates who I can reassign to help you," offered Crocken. "And perhaps you can institute a sign-in sheet for everybody on filing duty?"

"Oh, I did that already, two days ago when I realized this was more than just simple sloppiness, but you know how they are."

Crocken thanked Ahraft for bringing the problem to his attention, and reiterated his promise to help, and then excused himself.

As he returned to the central stairwell, he tried to think who might have started two weeks ago, but he didn't remember any new Juniors taking the oath around that time. Could it be an older Junior who had only recently switched from street work to filing work? What made more sense? Incompetence? Or sabotage? But if sabotage, to what end? What would any executioner have to gain from wrecking the filing system?

# Prayer

Catt had been keeping a busy schedule. All day she would work with Lemmy at the Polypantheonic Temple. As soon as she finished there she would fetch her stolen executioner's disguise and make her way into the Executioner's Guild Hall and blend in with the small army of Junior Executioners working in the records room. She would spend hours pretending to file reports while reading as much as she could, and learning a great deal about how the guild conducted policing business. She had learned enough to carry out her impersonation with greater accuracy and less risk of being caught.

Then she would hide her disguise, and go to the palace to spend a few precious hours sleeping with Segna before going out to start it all again.

This routine kept her mind busy at all times, and she liked that. There was very little idle time to worry about what could go wrong.

Today, Catt found herself again carrying a bag of offerings to be burnt in the Smokefields. She was in a hurry. She wanted to finish with her temple work early. In the past few days she had noticed that the squat Senior Executioner who seemed to be nominally in charge of the records room was growing suspicious. They had been watching more carefully, and had brought out a sign in sheet, that made the Juniors mutter and complain. Catt had forged a false name on it, and she didn't want to risk going back to that room tonight, it was too risky– and if she was going to take risks, she should try some new explorations.

Catt was preoccupied by this, but not so much that she had forgotten about meeting with Jangley.

Catt looked up at the big central tent. The setting sun was reddening the column of smoke that rose from its volcanic peak.

She made her way to the entrance, and peered inside, looking for Provincial. She did not see him, but she could see the fire up above where she was certain that Jangley would be working.

She mounted the steps. "Hello!" she called cautiously, trying to let Jangley know she was coming. She wasn't worried about startling the golem, but she was conscious that advance warning might make the fire a little safer to approach.

She was able to see the silhouette of Jangley's head, a spider's web's center with the blazing bonfire behind it. She waited as close as she dared while Jangley rearranged some racks of glistening ribs, and then lowered themselves down to the platform.

"Catt apprentice priest." Jangley greeted her.

"Jangley master chef", Catt greeted them in the same style.

"You bring offerings to burn?" Jangley queried.

"Yes," Catt replied.

"Bring tray," Jangley suggested.

Catt left the bag of offerings on the platform, and went back down the steps to search for the mesh tray that Provincial had used before. She found it easily, and brought it back up the steps.

Together they arranged the offerings on the tray. Catt got the feeling that Jangley could have done it much more quickly without her in the way of their many nimble wire limbs, but the golem seemed to want her participation. "You put. I help," Jangley said.

As Jangley lifted the tray up into the flames, Catt cleared her throat and said, "You asked me for a prayer last time I was here…"

Jangley's single eye seemed to refocus on her. "Yes. To the sun," they confirmed.

Catt took a piece of paper out of her shirt and unfolded it.

"*Don't pray to the sun with words,*" she read.

"*Words are for us, words are for stories,*"

"*The sun cannot hear our words,*"

Some of Jangley's wires formed spirals as they seemed to listen.

"*Pray to the sun with your actions,*"

"*Pray to the sun by being dependable,*"

"*Pray by rising every day as it does,*"

"*And walking your path under the sky,*"

"*And shining your own light on those around you,*"

*"Without asking for anything in return,"*
*"We can give nothing to the sun,"*
*"But we can try to be like it."*

After she had finished, Jangley just hung there a while, seeming to stare at her.

The fire above crackled and roared.

Catt felt awkward in the silence. She stared back at Jangley, unwilling to cast her eyes down. Had she missed the mark?

Finally Jangley moved, vibrating for just an instant with a dull twang, but still they said nothing.

"I am aware of the hypocrisy of saying *'Don't pray with words'* and then writing the whole prayer with words," Catt admitted, feeling her confidence falter, "but I thought that part was important, and I couldn't think of a way to write it without words."

Jangley twanged again, and then spoke, "I am thinking about this prayer. I will continue to think about it. Thank you Catt apprentice priest."

Catt exhaled, feeling more relieved than she had expected to feel.

"May I make it a part of me?" Jangley asked.

"Um... yes?" Catt was uncertain of what that meant.

A single wire appendage extended.

Catt realized that Jangley wanted the paper. She held it out, and the wire coiled smoothly around it, lifting it from her fingers.

Other wires redoubled back to Jangley's own head, and began to unscrew one end of the cylinder. The prayer was nimbly rolled up and tucked inside, and Jangley resealed their head with Catt's words inside.

After saying goodbye to the golem, and walking away from the Smokefields, Catt felt elated that her prayer had been accepted. Catt felt a purpose taking shape in her heart. She wanted to be a priest of many gods, but she also wanted to be a priest of things that were not gods. And she wanted Segna to have the chance to live long enough to see her do it.

Tonight, when she went back to the Executioner's Guild Hall, it was time to take a new risk.

# Armory

Someone was unlocking the armory door.

Catt slowed her pace, and tried so hard to be inconspicuous that it was like she was willing herself to be invisible.

He pushed the door open, and went inside… and left the door ajar!

Catt sped up. She wanted to see inside. The armory featured in many of the reports she had read, but it was always locked.

She glanced back casually and saw that nobody was in the hallway behind her. She peered through the crack of the open door. She could see the back of the executioner who had opened it receding away. He was not going to close it behind him!

Without further thought, she slipped silently through the door. If she was caught she would have to make up a lie about being lost. It was a risk she could take.

He didn't hear her. He didn't turn around.

Catt looked around frantically for a place to hide. There were some chairs, and a fletching table littered with feathers. There was a big rack of longbows and another of crossbows. None of them would conceal her. The chairs might suffice for a game of hide and seek with a child, but they were not good enough for this situation.

The only directions she could go were back out the door, or deeper into the armory.

The executioner still had not looked back. Catt decided. She followed.

There was a rack of axes, a rack of spears, a rack of even larger axes. There were shelves full of masks. The bottom shelf had wooden shields stacked on it.

Swiftly and silently Catt removed her own axe and placed it gently on one of the racks. It was too unwieldy. It would make noise if she let it hit the stone floor.

The moment she was rid of the axe, Catt dropped to the ground and wriggled underneath the low shelf with the shields on it. The shelf itself was slatted, but the shields provided an opaque ceiling she could hide beneath. She pressed herself all the way up against the wall in the darkness.

She could hear the footsteps still receding. She had done it! She was in!

Catt permitted herself a glance out to check on her axe. It wasn't the same kind of axe as the other ones on the rack, but it did not stand out. She felt that it would go unnoticed.

As she pulled her head back into the shadow, she accidentally let her mask strike against the stone. It made a sharp wooden clack.

The footsteps stopped.

Catt held her breath.

The footsteps started up again. They were returning towards her!

Catt silently rolled her eyes and mouthed a wordless curse.

The footsteps got closer.

Catt was running through possible lies in her head trying desperately to come up with a plausible sounding excuse for being here.

The man's feet stopped near her. She could see that he was wearing very high quality black boots with silvery trim. She could see black embroidery on the black fabric of the trouser legs. She had already been aware that the Seniors wore much nicer uniforms than the Juniors did, but up close, the clothes looked even more expensive than she would have guessed.

Catt didn't dare exhale.

The man's weight shifted as if he was looking around.

Then he abruptly started walking again, back towards the door.

A moment later, the door closed. She could hear a key turning in the lock. Could she dare to hope? He had gone out!

Catt breathed again. She waited to make sure it stayed quiet, but she was eager to come out and explore.

Just as Catt was about to come out of her hiding place, her eyes lit upon a spider. It was a small hairy thing tucked up between some scant strands of webbing in the corner of the underside of the shelf.

It was completely motionless except for one leg which it was waving.

Catt took pause. She stared at the tiny spider's leg. She imagined that the body language of the little creature was saying "Wait! Wait!"

Catt froze. She didn't need to be in a hurry. She settled her weight as much as she could into a comfortable position without making a sound. She breathed carefully and evenly, and countered her heartbeats, waiting for them to slow a little.

A long time went by, enough that Catt started to feel cold. She felt ready now to get out of her hiding place.

The spider was still there, still waving just one leg. As her eyes refocused on it, the footsteps started up again! Catt was so startled that it was all she could do to keep from flinching in surprise.

Moving decisively, the boots clicked past her hiding place, and away, deeper into the armory.

Catt's head reeled. The Senior Executioner had not gone out, he had been standing motionless just inside the door all that time! Had he been waiting for another noise?

Now his footsteps moved away, growing more and more distant, giving her a hint as to how large this armory really was.

Finally the footsteps were far enough away that she had to strain to hear them. There was a creak and a faint thud. It could have been another door, but Catt was not sure. Then silence.

Catt couldn't bring herself to trust this silence. Even when the spider stopped waving its little omen, lowered itself on a strand of silk, and scuttled away, Catt couldn't bring herself to exit her hiding place.

# Waiting Up

Segna waited up.

She had already finished her dinner, and her dessert, and her nightly note-taking. She was waiting for Catt to arrive.

Catt had come to see her every night since the night she had climbed over the balcony. They had not spoken again of the idea of *"saving"* her, but Segna surmised that Catt was probably still thinking about it, and was just keeping her promise not to let it come between them.

An extra dessert pastry was cooling on a plate on the little table, just in case Catt wanted it when she arrived.

With her note-taking complete, Segna put away her journal, and found one of her books of magic to read.

The big chair felt so empty now when she curled up in it alone. She browsed the spells distractedly. She wondered what would happen to her books when she was dead. Would they go back to the university? Could she give them to Catt? She would like that, but she was loath to bring up the topic.

Today was the first day of the fourth month. She had two more months to live. This morning the Chief Admonisher had advised her to start the process of selecting an undertaker. She would be expected to have decided on her interment instructions before the first day of the fifth month.

Some past version of herself would have expected this to be an easy decision. A cremation in the Smokefields, and an urn in an alcove among the rocks on the slopes of the mountain, the same way her guardians had been put to rest when they passed away.

In fact, the logistics of it were still that simple. Her wishes hadn't changed. What had changed was that she was thinking of Catt's feelings now. Segna knew Catt didn't accept the inevitability of her fate. Would talking about this be a wedge between them? Or would it be the path to closure that they would both need. Should she ask Catt to carry her urn up the mountain? Or should she prepare to have their goodbyes some night before the festival, and then take back the Consort's Locket and command Catt to go away and live and love and move on and not look back?

The spellbook lay open unheeded on Segna's lap as she stared into the night sky beyond the balcony. There was a third possibility, one that she feared. What if one night, Catt just didn't come? What if she just moved on without being forced to? Some night had to be the last night, and it might be Catt, and not herself who chose which night that would be. It was the simplest possibility. It might be the most likely possibility.

The pastry on the plate slowly grew stale.

# Windfall

Catt was awakened by the chattering of her own teeth. She had no idea how long she had been asleep there under the shelf of shields, but the cold stone floor had sapped away all the warmth in her body.

Catt clambered out from her hiding place. The terror that had kept her there was momentarily forgotten.

The armory seemed darker than before. Whatever magical lamps had illuminated it before were dimmed now.

Hugging her arms around herself and shivering, Catt made her way back to the door. It was locked. There didn't seem to be any other mechanism besides the yawning keyhole to open it from the inside.

Catt tried to think positively. She hadn't been caught. There was probably another way out. She now had plenty of opportunity to explore the armory.

Moving around seemed like the best way to get warm. Catt walked. The overall layout of the room seemed to be one long path, zig-zagging occasionally, with many smaller side paths going in between the shelves and racks.

The further back into the room she ventured the stranger the things on the shelves got. There were some rather exotic and impractical looking weapons, and some weapons and armor that seemed to be designed for people much larger than Catt. She remembered the huge ogre who had released her from prison months ago, but some of these swords and helmets looked too big even for the biggest person she had seen in the city. Many of these items were very dusty, and although some weapons, like the axes, seemed gleaming and sharp, others were rusty. She wondered if this room was at least partially just a storage place for weapons that had been confiscated from criminals over the years.

Finally Catt reached the end of the path. The main aisle just ended against a blank wall with an ornate but decaying horse blanket hung on it. There was a large box full of black capes with hoods. Catt thought about putting one on for extra warmth, but they were covered in a layer of fuzzy dust, so she decided against it.

She was about to turn around and head back the other way when she noticed something unusual. It was a tall cabinet made of polished wood, it had fine carvings on the sides, but they were half obscured in layers of fluffy dust. It had glass doors, like something that might be used to display fine porcelain in some noble's dining hall. All the other shelving in the armory was very plain and utilitarian. This one looked out of place.

Catt approached it, and peered through the glass. In the darkness, and through the smattering of dust that opaqued the glass, it was hard to see inside, but it seemed empty.

No, not empty... there was a gold-colored rod resting on a black velvet pillow on the bottom of the display case.

It was the wand.

Catt breathed deeply. "Praise all the gods!" she murmured. She spun in a circle. "All of them!"

She tried the handles. The glass doors were locked. There was a tiny keyhole. She might try picking the lock if she could find tools small enough.

The glass would be easy enough to break, but she decided she would rather not leave such obvious signs of tampering. She pressed the glass gently. It rattled slightly, being loose in the wooden framing, but she wasn't sure she could pry it out without breaking it.

After prodding and testing the glass doors for a while, Catt got an idea. She carefully pulled the whole cabinet away from the wall. The back of the thing was very plain. Spiders scattered. The wood was less finished here. It lacked the polish and detail that the front of the cabinet had, it was just one big panel.

Catt's fingers found the seam in the wood, and she pulled. The back panel creaked. Like the glass in the doors, this part was a bit loose too, probably with age and neglect. She changed her grip, and kept working on it. She could see small nails pulling out. The gap widened, until, after removing a few of the nails completely, she was able to squeeze her arm inside, and reach the wand.

She lifted it gingerly, and drew it out of the cabinet. It was golden in color, and seemed free of dust and corrosion. The wand felt cold in her hands, and she realized now that she was no longer cold herself. The excitement of finding it, and the exertion of extracting it had warmed her up considerably.

She lifted the wand and rotated it, looking at it from every side. It was not very heavy in her hand, so she guessed it must not really be made of gold.

Catt remembered seeing this wand in action. She remembered sitting there in shock, with Segna holding both her hands, and watching an executioner wield it over the body of the previous king. She remembered that he had spoken...

"*Activate!*", said Catt in Arashan.

The wand hummed. "**Reveal Enchantments?**" It asked in an otherworldly voice.

Catt's heart raced. "*Yes!*" she confirmed.

The hum changed to a lower pitch, and a white light radiated for a moment from the air around the wand.

For the span of a breath, nothing happened, and then the wand announced; "**Failure**," as it went dark.

Of course, there was nothing magical nearby for the wand to detect, so that made sense.

Catt gazed at the wand for a while longer. Now what? She had found it, she had stolen it, and she had figured out how to activate it. But how was she supposed to tamper with it? How did this advance her goal of saving Segna's life?

Finally, Catt tucked the wand into her belt. She would take it with her. She would have to figure out how to sneak it back in here another time.

She pushed the cabinet back up against the wall. She had disturbed its dust, but for the most part it looked as it had before. This was certainly far less conspicuous than if she had smashed the glass.

Catt picked up a few of the nails she had loosened from the back of the cabinet, and took them with her as she made her way back to the entrance.

At the door, Catt made use of the nails and set about trying to pick the lock. It took a long time, and she had to be careful not to make too much noise that might be heard from the hallway outside. By the time she got the last tumbler to give way, the muscles in her hands were aching painfully. She had visibly scratched up the keyhole, and had loosened the whole mechanism inside, but it was opened. She had to hope it would still accept its key, and that the damage she had done to it was not so bad it would draw unwanted scrutiny, but if she was lucky, and nobody noticed it and replaced the lock, then she was pretty confident she could pick it again much more easily next time.

Catt stepped out into the hallway, and closed the door casually behind her. A pair of executioners were walking down the hallway, discussing something between themselves. They didn't take any notice of Catt or where she had just come from. Of course she was supposed to be there! Of course there was nothing to see here!

Catt made her way out of the Guild Hall, making sure to keep the wand concealed in her cape. Outside, the sun was rising over the mountains. It was morning already.

# Disassembly

Segna's stomach had felt sour all day. She had tried to rush through her meetings. She had lost her temper with her advisors and argued with them. She had left dinner early, even though doing so had probably offended the Ambassador from Succour.

Not even resting submerged in the pool in the royal bath-house made her feel better. It just made her feel even more alone. Maybe she was despairing for nothing. Maybe Catt would come tonight, with some story of whatever mischief had kept her away last night. But maybe she wouldn't. Segna understood that it was out of her hands. Either she would see Catt again, or she wouldn't... but the idea of spending her final two months without her seemed unbearably depressing.

Segna drained her bath, and dressed in a silk robe and went to her big chair on the balcony. She scribbled in her journal for a while. She hadn't accomplished very much today, but she knew it was important to write something. This routine was important, and it wouldn't do to let it fall apart. She was determined not to let herself fall apart. She would be a good King, even if maybe she had to do it alone.

Still, she was hoping for a knock on the door. She couldn't help but hope. She thought about how stubbornly Catt had clung to the idea of helping her escape her fate, and in that moment, it seemed more forgivable than it had before.

Suddenly a strange voice came from somewhere behind Segna. She couldn't make out the words. Segna craned her head around the back of the chair and looked, caught somewhere between confusion and alarm. The voice had come from one of her side rooms, the enormous walk-in closet where she kept her boxes of books. Was one of the servants in there? Why would they be there now? And why had they sounded so strange?

A different voice spoke. It spoke a single word, which sounded like the confirmation word of a magical spell. It sounded like Catt's voice!

Segna jumped up and ran to the door.

Catt was sitting on the floor with her back up against one of the boxes. Half a dozen books were spread out open around her. In her hands was a golden wand. Hazy white light was radiating from it.

"**Failure**," said the wand.

Catt smiled at her as if nothing was unusual about this tableau. "I didn't break it!" she announced cheerfully.

"Catt? What are you doing?" Segna asked, pushing aside one of the books and kneeling next to her. She felt bewildered, but her heart was also light as a feather. Seeing Catt's face made her feel as if a heavy burden had been lifted off her shoulders.

"I've been trying to figure this thing out," said Catt, brandishing the wand. "This stuff is not easy! But I did figure out how to take it apart and put it back together." Catt began to unscrew one end of the wand.

"How long have you been in here?" Segna asked.

"Almost all day," said Catt, "I let myself in this morning," removing the end-cap of the wand, Catt began to very carefully extract the rolled up strips of vellum inside.

Segna's jaw hung open at the realization that while she had spent the whole day worrying that Catt might never come back, here she had been, right here in her own rooms. She wasn't sure if she felt angry or comforted.

"I just dumped these out the first time," Catt was saying. "It took me forever to read enough to get them back in the right order."

"Wait, wait," Segna said, "back up, explain. What is going on here?"

"I'm trying to understand how this wand works, so I can modify it," said Catt, her eyes practically gleaming with excitement, "and I feel free to say I am really glad you are here. This stuff is over my head, and I need your help."

"But why?... where did?..." Segna started at the strange wand, still not grasping what this was all about. Only when she looked into Catt's eyes did realization dawn on her. Catt was so excited, as if... as if...

Segna looked at the wand again. The Wand. She recognized it now. Her eyes grew wide. "How did you get this!?"

"A little luck, and a lot of sneakiness!" Catt beamed with pride.

"Oh, no, no!" Segna murmured, trying to wrap her head around the implications.

"Don't worry," Catt reassured, "Nobody knows that I have it."

Segna tried to protest, but she couldn't find the words. She watched in mute shock as Catt placed the empty wand on one of the books, and arranged the little rolls of vellum neatly on the floor.

"I can read parts of the ones on this end," Catt was saying, "I know they have something to do with the voice activation, but these other ones? Woo! How does anyone even write that small?"

Segna began to shiver. She was imagining executioners cutting Catt apart.

Catt seemed to notice. She pushed the vellum away carefully, keeping them in order, and scooted over to Segna, moving another book out of the way.

Segna felt Catt's arms wrap around her and squeeze, strong but gentle.

"Don't be afraid," said Catt.

"How can I not be!?" Segna pleaded.

Catt didn't reply.

Segna buried her face into Catt's shoulder.

"Imagine this," said Catt, "we fake your death..."

Segna shook her head in disbelief, still leaning into Catt's hug. "Faking my own death is supposed to make me feel better?"

"Yes! Hear me out," Catt said, caressing the back of Segna's neck, "When the executioners come to verify that you are really dead–that's what they'll do, right?"

Segna nodded.

"Right," Catt continued, "they'll use this to verify that you aren't an illusion."

Segna nodded again. Catt's words were anything but comforting, but her voice and her embrace were very comforting.

"But you *will* be an illusion, and they won't know it, because we'll have modified the wand so it *won't* detect the magic."

Segna lifted her head and looked into Catt's eyes.

"And you and I can leave, and they won't be hunting you down, because they won't know you are still alive."

"Catt..."

"Yes?" Catt answered, eyes brimming with optimism.

"If a King dies before the year is over, the executioners do use the wand to verify the body is real, then they behead it."

Catt nodded, "Which won't matter, since it will be an illusion."

Segna continued, "Then they would have the head sewn back on, and they would save the body until the Regicide festival, and then they would behead it a second time for the ceremony."

Catt frowned, "Yeah... that sounds like them, actually."

"I saw it once when I was young," Segna explained, "we had a King who died of a bad heart in his first month."

Catt grimaced.

"I don't think I can make an illusion that will hold up for that long," Segna admitted.

Catt nodded grimly.

Segna continued... "But if we just waited for the Regicide festival, the illusion would only have to last for one night..." She had just meant to explain to Catt why it wouldn't work, and now she was feeling herself pulled into the idea.

"You could do it!" Catt exclaimed. Her eyes seemed to burn with exuberance.

"An illusion of a person that looks real, and feels solid, and moves realistically is a difficult spell, but yes, I think I could do it. You would have to go with it to guide it and sit next to it at the festival while I would escape and hide... and I would have to make sure that it would react convincingly to being beheaded... and the illusion would only have to last long enough to get to the crematorium..."

Catt squeezed her again. "We can do this together!"

Segna felt strange. This was the first time she had allowed herself to imagine the possibility of a life after kingship.

"May I kiss you?" asked Catt.

"Okay," Segna replied, letting her muscles relax.

After a long slow kiss they both looked at the disassembled wand.

"What about the wand?" Catt asked.

Segna picked up one of the strips of vellum from the middle of the arrangement. She looked at it.

The spell etched onto the surface was incredibly complex. She would need a magnifying glass just to read it. The self-contemplative focus etchings looked like interlacing snowflakes.

"This isn't going to be easy either," Segna said. "Wand spells are among the most difficult because they have to be written in such a way as to be self-contained. They have to work even if the user knows nothing about the spell– even if the user knows nothing about magic in general. It's very advanced sorcery, and I'll have to do it quickly if you're going to be able to put this back where you found it before anyone notices it missing."

"From the dust where I found it," Catt said, "I have a feeling that nobody touches it between uses."

"That's good," acknowledged Segna, "but we shouldn't rely on it," she put down the vellum and examined another one.

"Surely writing a spell that doesn't detect magic is a whole lot easier than writing one that does detect it?" Catt suggested.

Segna shook her head. "We can't just replace the spell with one that doesn't work. What if they test the wand before the ceremony?"

"Oh," said Catt.

"Instead I'll need to decipher the existing spell enough to insert an exception to it."

"Like it won't work on illusions? But works on other spells?" Catt asked

"Or maybe I could add a command word that disables it temporarily?" Segna offered.

"And I could say it when they behead the illusion!" Catt clapped with glee.

This plan was difficult, and dangerous for both of them if anything should go wrong, but Segna had been infected with Catt's optimism. It was not impossible, and together, as a team, they could do it.

# Lost Axe

Crocken stood looming over Ex-Junior Executioner Fullbrite.

Fullbrite's father had offered him a chair, but Crocken had declined to sit in it.

Fullbrite cowered on the middle of a floral-patterned sofa. Her knees were tucked up against her chest, and her right hand, the one with the bandages, was clenched by her heart. Her maskless face seemed full of anger and determination, but did not make eye contact..

Crocken held two axes, one in each hand. His own, and Fullbrite's.

"Yes, it's mine," Fullbrite managed to say.

"Do you wish to revise your previous statement?"

Fullbrite shook her head furiously. "No, I told the truth," she said with just a note of defiance, that was tempered by hiccups.

"Then why was it found in the armory?"

"I don't know!" said Fullbrite.

Crocken said nothing.

"Was my mask there?" Fullbrite asked.

"Was it?" Crocken repeated.

Fullbrite glared at him angrily.

"You have nothing to add?" Crocken prompted.

Fullbrite stared at her axe.

Crocken could hear Fullbrite's parents shifting uncomfortably on the couch behind him. He did not look at them. They were petty aristocrats, well mannered enough to know not to interrupt guild business.

"I've been thinking..." Fullbrite began.

Crocken nodded silently to encourage her to continue.

"I was walking with a friend the night my things were stolen," Fullbrite looked at the arm of the couch as she spoke, "And she was the only person who saw where I hid them... I've been looking for her, and I can't find her. I think she was the one who took them."

"Could you identify her?"

"Maybe?" Fullbrite frowned, "Her name is Nora. She has red hair... and little horns that she hid under a scarf."

"Could you sketch her face?"

Fullbrite shook her head, "She had a mask on."

"An executioner?" asked Crocken. This seemed like the lead he was looking for.

"No," said Fullbrite, "just a mask like some people wear. Not one of ours."

"I thought you said this was a friend?" Crocken said, "but you never saw her face?"

Fullbrite shrugged.

After a silence, she asked, "What are you going to do to me?"

Crocken had actually not come to do anything but ask questions, but he did not feel the need to tell her that. She had already paid the price for breaking her guild vow, and there wasn't enough evidence to connect her with the disappearance of the wand other than the strange coincidence of finding her axe in the armory more than two weeks after it had been reported stolen.

"If you see this Nora again, let us know," said Crocken.

Fullbrite nodded. She was looking at the axe now. "Can I have it back?" she pleaded.

"No," said Crocken.

# Drugs

Catt looked around *Pulp Scribe*. The selection of pamphlets and periodicals had changed, but the shop looked the same. She was again the only customer.

The clerk looked at her curiously.

"Hi," Catt said in greeting, "I'm looking for some drugs."

The clerk grinned. "I remember you, I knew you looked like a Reff-head. How much you want?"

"No," Catt said with a fake smile, "I'm actually more interested in the Forget-me-yes."

"Oh-ho, you're into that kinda stuff," the clerk leered lewdly, "You want the petals or the concentrate?"

"The concentrate, please, I think." Catt replied.

"They're two Shmouds per vial, but the vials are kinda small," the clerk held up the tip of their little finger.

"Uh... okay," Catt made a show of checking her coin purse, which was fuller than usual since Segna had given her some money for this expedition. "I guess I'll take three then."

"Ooh, big spender," the clerk chuckled. "Okay, wait here while I get it. Just pretend to read a book or something."

"Or I could actually read a book?" Catt suggested.

"Whatever," and the clerk disappeared through the curtain to the back room.

Catt leaned against the counter and flipped briefly through a copy of **Lizard Cannibals Revealed** and then threw it back on the shelf.

Segna had been spending every spare moment working on deciphering the wand's spells. She still had to carry on with her Royal duties to keep up appearances, which left little time for sleep. Catt had been staying up to watch her and absorb as much as she could, but there wasn't a lot she could do to help, so she had taken it upon herself to plan the other parts of the escape. After creating the illusion of herself, Segna would need a safe path out of the palace without being seen. Catt had devised a pretty good one that only required a bare minimum of climbing, but it wasn't foolproof. She needed the doses of Forget-me-yes so that if Segna was unlucky enough to bump into a servant or a groundskeeper on her way out of the palace, she could dose them, and get out without hurting anyone, just leaving them a little confused.

Coming up with back-up plans and emergency contingencies helped soothe Catt's nerves, and made her feel like she was contributing to the escape plan while she waited however long it was going to take until it was time to return the wand to the armory.

The clerk returned with a paper sack. They showed Catt the three tiny sealed vials.

"Wanna uncork one and smell it?" the clerk asked. "You know, to make sure it's good?"

"Ha-ha," Catt said wryly, acknowledging the joke, but not laughing at it.

She handed over the Shmouds.

"Pleasure doing business with you, I never saw you, you were never here," said the clerk. "Come back when you change your mind about the Reff."

# Difficulty

Catt returned to the palace after a few hours of helping Lemmy with temple work. She wished she could say something to prepare him for the fact that she would be vanishing at the end of the year. She loved being an acolyte, and she respected the example of priesthood and service that Lemmy had shown to her. She would miss the Polypantheonic Temple, certainly, but when she weighed it on the scale of her heart against a life with Segna, there was no contest. She would have to disappear suddenly, and telling anyone else about it seemed to add unnecessary risk to an already risky enterprise.

In the palace dining hall, Catt found the advisors dining without Segna.

"She excused herself without eating a bite," sniffed the Steward of Precedent.

"Do you think she is taking ill?" asked the Chief Admonisher.

"I don't know," answered Catt, "maybe she is feeling stressed? Have you all been stressing her out with too much King-business?"

"No more than usual," replied the Steward of Precedent.

"Isn't soothing her stress *your* job?" the Chief Admonisher asked with eyebrows waggling.

Catt ignored this. "I'll take up a plate of food and see if I can get her to eat something," she said.

As Catt carried two plates up the steps to Segna's Chambers, she worried about how much pressure Segna was putting on herself to figure out the necessary wand modifications. If they didn't solve it soon, Segna's distraction might draw unwanted scrutiny from the advisors. Still, it seemed unavoidable. The wand was the crux of their plan.

Catt let herself in, and put the food on the table by the balcony.

Catt looked in the book closet, but Segna wasn't there. "Segna?"

"In here!" Segna replied.

Catt went into the bedroom, and found Segna on a stepladder that servants used when cleaning. She was prying one of the magical lanterns off the wall. A small heap of glowing lanterns was piled on the edge of the bed.

"Can you help me with these?" Segna asked. She did look tired and stressed. Her eyes were a little bloodshot.

"What are we doing?" Catt asked, moving the ladder to the next lamp.

"Testing something," Segna said. "I'm about at my wit's end."

"How about if we stop and eat first?" suggested Catt.

Segna shook her head. "This won't take long."

It took a while to get all the lights down and into the pile. The room looked strange with all the illumination concentrated into one spot.

"Check outside, please," Segna asked.

Catt went to the door and verified that no servants had come into the balcony room while they had been working. Segna had been growing more paranoid about someone walking in on them.

Segna took the wand out from where she had hidden it under the blankets.

"*Activate!*" Segna said.

"***Reveal Enchantments?***" hummed the wand.

"*Confirm!*" said Segna.

White light glowed from the wand, seeming dim in comparison to the jumble of magic lanterns.

"***Failure,***" announced the wand.

Segna stomped her foot, and seemed ready to throw the wand.

Catt steadied her hand. "It's okay, what was that supposed to do?"

"Detect the enchantments!" Segna said, sounding exasperated. "That was the original spell! It has all the original vellums, in the correct order. I haven't modified any of them yet!"

Catt took ahold of Segna and steered her towards the door. "Let's eat first, then we can talk about it."

Segna yielded, but said, "I have to hide the wand first."

"I'll do it," Catt offered.

After the wand was secreted away in the book room, Catt found Segna crumpled on the big chair, nibbling listlessly at a bit of tree lobster.

Catt sat with her shoulder against Segna's and they ate in silence for a few minutes.

"I started with testing it on one lamp," said Segna, "and I thought maybe the enchantment in just one was too weak."

Catt nodded. That explained the pile of lamps.

Segna continued, "but it always says '*Failure*', and that's not what it says at the Regicide ceremony."

"It's not?" asked Catt, trying to remember what it had said the one time she had really seen it in action.

"No," said Segna. "It doesn't say anything! It glows and then the body glows, and that's it!"

"What if it needs a body to work on?" Catt suggested.

"Maybe?" Segna considered, "I should go cross reference the focus diagrams against the kind used in necromancy..." Segna started to get up out of the chair.

"Hold on," Catt said, holding on to her, "please finish eating. Rest a little, we have enough time, and you'll think better afterwards."

## Suspect

"Sir, have a look at this."

Crocken looked up from his reports to see Senior Executioner Brace, and a Junior he didn't recognize.

"Is it important?" Crocken sighed. He had been following leads on the wand investigation all day, and he was ready to go home and get his mask off.

"It's relevant, sir," said Brace. They placed a piece of paper on Crocken's desk.

It was a sketch of a woman's face. His first thought was that she looked suspicious. There were some notes scribbled around the margins. An arrow pointing to her hair led from the word "Red". She had small horns.

"Oh, you found one," said Crocken. This was what he had asked Brace to look for this morning.

"Actually, it just arrived today," said Brace. "It came from one of our entrapment informants. She bought three doses of an illegal drug."

Crocken stared at the eyes in the drawing. "This seems only mildly relevant," said Crocken.

Crocken hadn't told Brace why he was looking for a suspect who fit this description. The Reaper had instructed that although the wand investigation was top priority, it should proceed discreetly until more information had been collected.

"Tell him, Thana," said Brace.

The Junior Executioner spoke up. "Sir, I know her! I've been on palace guard duty, and she has been there every day! I think this is the King's Consort!"

Crocken sat up straighter. That was interesting. All day his investigations had felt like dead ends and grasping at straws. What did it mean if the King's Consort vaguely resembled the description Fullbrite had given him of the person who stole her axe, and that axe was found near the place where the wand disappeared. Maybe it meant nothing?

Crocken read the notes at the bottom of the sketch.

*"Bought 3 doses Forget. 6 Shmouds. Refused Reff. Two weeks ago bought Chilling Tales of Faithless Kings"*

Crocken re-read the last two words, *"Faithless Kings"*

The pieces seemed to line up in his head. He had no proof, just a tenuous chain of suspicion, but one that needed to be followed, and urgently.

# Necromancy

Catt woke up on the big chair. Segna was gone. She had convinced Segna to finish eating, and then Segna had meditated until they had both fallen asleep. Now it was night, Catt wasn't sure how late it was.

Catt got up, and went to the book closet. Segna was there. She had relocated some of the lamps they had taken down from the bedroom, and laid them out on the floor. The wand was there, and the strips of vellum were on the floor. Segna was poised over one of them with a magnifying glass.

"Hey," said Catt, softly.

"It does use necromancy!" Segna said, glancing up and gesturing for Catt to come closer.

Catt stepped over a book and crouched down to look.

"I didn't recognize it before, it's not my area of expertise, but I have figured out a lot!"

Catt could hear the excitement in Segna's voice, she was talking fast. Besides the excitement there was something else. Fear?

"The wand does search for a nearby dead body," Segna continued, "and it has to be dead, or it can't proceed, and this part is strange— it has checks for leadership."

"So it only works on dead Kings?"

"Yes," Segna nodded, "I'm sure of it, I have read about that sort of thing before, there are legendary spells like that, but it is very advanced warmagic, like what would be used to target a general but bypass the soldiers. I don't understand why they would include something so complex but so unnecessary!"

"But that's good for us, right?" Catt reasoned. "It means they can't test it in advance. It means you don't have to keep it working, you can just gut the spell and replace the whole thing with a simple fake right?"

Segna nodded, but she looked worried, "There is more. I was able to decipher more of the spell once I realized it was necromancy and not detection... these ones..." Segna indicated the last four vellums, "are all about trapping a soul. This wand doesn't do what we thought it did. It drains the soul out of the dead King's body... They were going to take my soul with this!"

Catt took Segna's hand and held it tight.

"Does that mean that all spirits of all the old kings are trapped in there?" Catt asked, staring at the wand.

"I don't think so," Segna said, "I found another command word here," she gave Catt the magnifying glass, and held up the last vellum.

Catt looked. Segna pointed it out to her.

"It looks like *Disgorge*," Catt said, studying the tiny script.

"Yes," said Segna, "and the lines of focus there are incomplete. It looks like it is supposed to be connected to another artifact in order for that part of the spell to work."

Catt let the magnifying glass hang limp in her hand, and she sat quietly for a moment absorbing this information.

Finally she said, "That means that even if we can get away with fooling them with your illusion, they'll find out it is a fake eventually, when they realize they can't disgorge your soul into wherever they plan to put it."

Segna nodded, her face grim.

"We'll still have enough time to escape," Catt said.

"And they'll be coming after us," Segna added.

Catt and Segna looked into each other's eyes. There was no question about it, they still had to go through with this, even more urgently now than ever.

# Apprehension

There was a distant pounding on the door.

Segna startled. It sounded considerably more forceful than the way the servants knocked.

Catt said, "You hide the wand, I'll see who it is."

"Yes," Segna nodded. She began rapidly but carefully re-rolling the vellums and putting them back into the wand. It would be nothing, she told herself, but her hands still shook as she worked.

She finished screwing the gold end-cap back on, and was about to stuff the wand deep into one of the boxes, when she heard a voice from the other room.

"Catt Zago, we have an emergency warrant for your arrest. Cooperate and you will not be harmed."

Segna's blood ran cold.

"This has to be a mistake," said Catt, "What's this about?"

Segna could not see what was happening outside in the balcony room, but she could hear the tension coiled in Catt's voice.

"You are being arrested for violation of your probation, and you are to be questioned in connection to an ongoing investigation."

"Where is the King?" demanded another voice. Segna thought it might be the Visor of Protocol.

It dawned on her that the book box was not an adequate hiding place for the wand. She looked around desperately for something better. The room was mostly bare other than the books, and a few hangers full of clothing.

"You can't be serious, I haven't done anything," protested Catt, adding, "Her Majesty is asleep. Can't this nonsense wait until morning?"

Segna whispered the words of an illusion to render a small object invisible. Even before she finished the hand gestures, she knew the spell was going to fail. The lines of focus twisted and warped in the presence of the much stronger ones inside the wand. It did not even flicker invisible for a single second.

"You will now consent to be restrained," said the first voice. It spoke calmly and with authority. "You may have your court-appointed intercessor present for your questioning."

"I don't consent to that!" said Catt angrily.

Segna tried desperately to think of another way to hide the wand. Did she know a spell that could stick it to the ceiling? It would be less likely to fail, but it would be useless if someone just looked up.

"What happened in here? Your majesty!? Where are you!?" Segna was more sure now that the voice was that of the Visor.

"What happened to the lights?"

That last voice sounded like the Chief Admonisher. They must have looked in the bedroom. Segna had not put any of the lamps back up on the walls, they would still be in a messy pile.

Segna thought about her special teleportation spell. If only she could send the wand through the floor, but of course, it didn't work that way. It only worked on one's living self. It couldn't even take clothing along. Writing a version of the spell that worked on an inanimate magical object would be the work of many hours, even days.

"Restrain her by force," said the first voice.

"Yes Sir," said two other voices in unison.

Helping Catt suddenly felt more urgent than hiding the wand. Segna returned to her original idea. She crammed the golden rod deep into the book box, and hastily pushed books over it.

She stepped out of the door and said, in her most regal voice, "What is the meaning of this!?"

Two executioners were advancing on Catt. Their axes were still on their belts, one was tall with unusually long arms, the other was barrel-chested with broad shoulders and carried a pair of manacles. A third executioner was standing back watching cooly. A clipboard was in his hand. His uniform looked different than the others, and he had a fringe of greying beard peeking out under the edge of his mask.

Catt had positioned the table and chair between herself and the approaching executioners. Her posture was taut as if ready to pounce. She had one hand on the back of the oversized chair, as if she was preparing to wield the heavy furniture as a weapon.

"I command you to stop!" ordered Segna.

The two executioners hesitated, but the third said, "You don't have authority to command us directly, Your Majesty, that requires an act of the courts."

"It's true!" piped in the Seneschal of Delays. Several of Segna's advisors were clustered by her bedroom door. It looked like a couple more were outside in the hallway.

The executioners rounded the chair, one from each side. Catt vaulted up and over the chair, toppling the table as she landed. The remains of their dinner clattered to the floor, but one of the plates was already in Catt's hand and she was smashing it into the face of the long-armed executioner nearest the balcony. Before the shards of porcelain had even hit the ground, she lunged at the barrel-chested executioner with the manacles, punching them in the neck, directly below the mask. They crumpled to their knees, gurgling.

"Axes out!" barked the bearded executioner with the clipboard, adding, "Catt Zago, you have waived your right to a bloodless arrest."

The executioner by the balcony swung their axe viciously at Catt, but overextended. Catt leaped, planted one foot on the handle of the axe, and kicked the executioner's arm, causing them to drop the weapon and fall back against the railing. Catt surged forward and began trying to push them over the edge.

The executioner with the clipboard had discarded it, and was advancing towards Catt's back, axe upraised.

Segna screamed.

The axe missed by a breath as Catt spun out of the way, but the executioner with the manacles had recovered enough to kick the chair into her path. She toppled over with it, and they grabbed first her hair, and then her wrist, and twisted her arm behind her. Catt tore at the eyeholes of the barrel-chested executioner's mask, almost dislodging it from their face, but they continued twisting until she was pinned face down on the stone.

Meanwhile the bearded executioner had helped his long-armed ally back onto the right side of the railing. He lifted the axe again, aiming it at Catt's prone form.

"Stop!" Segna screamed, throwing herself between him and Catt.

He lowered the axe, stepped forward, and seized her wrist with an iron grip. "Restrain the King, please," he said over his shoulder.

Segna could see that Catt had already been manacled, and was still being pinned to the floor.

"Let her go!" Segna demanded. "I command you!"

The long-armed executioner's vice-like hands closed around Segna's wrist, and then an instant later, both her hands were trapped behind her back.

"I'm sorry, Your Majesty," said the bearded one who seemed to be the leader. "We may have started on the wrong foot. I am Senior Executioner Crocken, I am arresting your Consort, and no, you do not have the authority to stop me."

Segna glared at him, and then glanced imploringly at her advisors. None of them made any move to help. The Visor just shook their head, and the Admonisher stood with mouth hanging open.

Crocken picked up his clipboard from the floor as he continued, "Your interference is not helping her."

"You were about to kill her!" Segna spat, tugging at her restraints. She could hear Catt grunting with pain and exertion as she struggled unsuccessfully to free herself.

"We might still," said Crocken. Then to someone in the hallway he called, "Send for the backup, we'll need to search these rooms."

"Stop hurting her!" Segna shouted.

"You may hurt her less," Crocken said to the barrel-chested executioner.

Catt stopped struggling suddenly, and was still.

"What did you do?" Segna wailed.

"I'm okay," Catt said in a surprisingly calm voice.

"Don't let your guard down," Crocken ordered.

Three more executioners entered the room.

"We sent a runner to fetch Jantos," said one of them to Crocken.

"Good," replied Crocken. "Search these chambers."

"Who are we looking for?" they asked, glancing at Segna.

"*What*, not *Who*," Crocken corrected. "I'll tell you if you find it."

"What *are* you looking for?" Segna demanded, knowing exactly what he was looking for.

Crocken looked at her for a moment, but did not answer.

Then to the advisors, he said, "You all will need to wait in the hall," and he shooed them away from the bedroom and towards the door.

They complied sullenly with no resistance. Only the Chief Admonisher lingered just outside the door where Segna could still see them.

The executioners made a quick search of the rooms. Catt made no further noise. Segna stared blankly, her mind feeling numb.

"Sir! Is this it?" said one of the executioners, coming out of the book closet carrying the wand.

The executioner who was holding Segna's restraints sucked in their breath.

The Chief Admonisher emitted a low whistle.

"That's it. Good work," said Crocken, taking the wand.

He turned to look directly at Segna. In a loud voice, he said, "King Segna Ur-Segna, I find you Faithless to your royal vow, you will be slain according to protocol."

This was what Segna was expecting, she just had not expected it so suddenly. She had not expected it to happen right here and now.

"What about the High Court?" Segna asked. "Don't I get a trial?" She could see that her advisors were now crowded around the open door, all trying to peer in.

"Oh, yes," said Crocken in a serious tone, "there will be a trial. If they find that I should not have killed you, I will be severely disciplined."

Segna stared at the wand in Crocken's hand, her heart pounding. He had put his axe back on his belt when he had taken it. None of the other executioners were lifting their axes to strike her or Catt.

"So what happens now?" she demanded angrily.

"We need another Senior Executioner present," said Crocken. "It won't be long."

"Can you kill us quick?" asked Catt. Her voice seemed small.

Segna looked at Catt. The executioner had one knee on her back, pinning her down.

Crocken shook his head, "Protocol dictates that there is a specific pattern of cuts that we use for Faithless Kings and their accomplices. It won't be quick... but we won't drag it out either."

Segna shivered.

"Can we... have a minute together... to say goodbye?" asked Catt.

"So you can try to escape? No," said Crocken.

"Please! She won't," Segna implored.

Crocken seemed to be thinking about this. "Sit her up," he said. "You can say goodbye from where you are."

The barrel-chested executioner complied warily, easing off and letting Catt shift into a kneeling position. They moved carefully and seemed wary of being kicked at any moment, but the fight seemed to have gone out of Catt.

Segna stared into Catt's eyes. They burned with an intensity that was at odds with her defeated body language. Segna tried to move closer, and the executioner who held her allowed her a few steps so she would have been within arm's reach of Catt if either one of them had been able to use their arms. Segna choked back tears, wanting to shut out the rest of the world and remember only Catt's face, and think about nothing else around them or anything that was about to happen.

Catt began to speak;

*"To go away suddenly into the awayness- bringing only what makes my love my love- escaping the abyss towards exactly where I put my mind-"*

Segna realized that Catt was trying to recite her spell, the one tattooed on her body. She was unable to hold back the tears any longer. She knew Catt couldn't possibly make the spell work properly. If it did anything at all, it might fling her into the sky, or bury them down in the earth below.

*Wouldn't that be better?* She thought. If a failed teleportation spell embedded them into the rock under the palace, the executioners wouldn't be able to cut them apart. They wouldn't be able to steal her soul with that horrible wand.

Segna let the lines of focus flow through her mind. She started to speak the words along with Catt, saying the words that Catt missed, speaking variables into being, helping to complete the spell.

"What are they doing?" asked one of the executioners.

"I don't know," said Crocken. "Stop them."

# Together

Catt felt a burgeoning unreal prickle, much stronger than the hands of the executioner grasping at her.

Everything except Segna went blindingly black as the two of them were sucked into a spaceless void. There was a confusing shapeless sensation of tumbling. Catt couldn't breathe.

Then suddenly the world rushed back again, and with a jolting whump, Catt felt her body flop onto a smooth flat stone floor.

It was dark, but this was only an ordinary darkness, like being in a cave with no candle. It was not like the void she had just passed through.

Catt's hands were free. The manacles were gone. Her clothes were gone too. Her wrists still hurt. Her fist still hurt from the fight. She could hear a sound like rapid breathing.

"Segna?" Catt asked.

"Catt? Are we dead?" Segna's voice was very close by.

"I don't think so. You're breathing... I'm breathing." Catt moved one hand up to her mouth to make sure.

"You did my spell!" Segna said.

"I love you," Catt said suddenly. It wasn't what she expected herself to say, but she knew it was true. She reached out and found Segna's face with her hands.

They pulled each other closer.

After a moment of holding each other tight, Segna said, "Are you certain we aren't dead?"

"Not completely," Catt admitted. "Can you magic up some light?"

Segna leaned back a bit, and worked a spell. As the words finished, a faint glow radiated from her hand. There she was.

Catt looked around. The floor they were sitting on was made of square tiles, tight fitting and smooth, as if worn down by age.

There were walls, also smooth, but with irregular shapes and organic flourishes, as if someone had carved and polished the limestone walls of a natural cavern.

"Where are we?" asked Catt.

"Maybe in the cellars of the palace?" Segna guessed. "My spell couldn't have taken us very far... and I was trying to aim it downward..."

"I was trying to aim us wherever the gods could take us so we could be together," said Catt.

"Oh, Catt," Segna said. Water glistened at the corners of her eyes in the faint light.

They embraced again.

After a long moment, they parted and looked into each other's eyes again.

Catt watched a tear drip sideways across the bridge of Segna's nose, and fly away horizontally to one side.

Segna reached up and touched her own nose with her glowing hand. Faint confusion registered on her face.

Catt reached out and caught another tear on her fingertip. She held it close to the light from Segna's hand, and they both stared at it.

The droplet of water leaned preposterously to one side, as if gravity was pulling it in a different direction than everything else.

"Magic?" Catt asked.

"Not a spell I know, but it must be magic," Segna confirmed.

Catt shook her finger gently, and the droplet broke free and leaped away into the darkness. Catt and Segna both turned their heads and looked in the direction it had gone.

"Let's go that way," suggested Catt.

They stood and walked hand in hand through the strange passage with its faceted and carved walls.

The light from Segna's hand illuminated a simple door set into the end of the passage. It looked old, but was profoundly ordinary. It seemed out of place.

Catt tentatively pulled the handle. It slid open with a soft creak. There did not seem to be any lock. Behind it was a narrow stair cut into the rock. It curved upward.

"If we really are in the cellars, this may lead up to the palace," Segna said.

Catt imagined the scene they must have left behind. Two piles of empty clothes, and the King and Consort spirited away. The executioners must be furious, and the palace must be in an uproar. "I'm not eager to go back there just yet," Catt opined.

"Nor am I," Segna agreed.

They both looked back the way they had come.

"Why would there be magic in the palace cellars that makes water fall sideways?" Segna pondered.

"Let's try going the other way," Catt suggested.

They followed the passage away from the door. Catt looked at the floors and walls as they went, trying to spot the exact place where they had started, but it was not easy to tell.

After a while, the passage widened, and the ceiling vanished upwards, too far away for the small light to reach. The floor remained smooth and flat.

There was something large and round ahead of them, a dark textured sphere, looming more than three times as high as their heads.

"What is that?" Catt asked.

"I have no idea," Segna said, hesitating.

Catt took a few steps to the side, craning her neck, trying to verify her estimate of the size of the thing. It seemed to be resting on a ring of stone the same color as the walls. There were markings on the floor, carved lines and rune-like shapes.

Segna was already examining the floor. Many lines seemed to converge at one point, spreading out from there, and surrounding the sphere.

"It's a spell..." Segna declared. She knelt, and began examining it, running her fingers over the carvings.

Catt stayed close to her, but stared up at the sphere. It was a mostly dark red material that looked to Catt like rusty iron. It was covered all over with small black triangles which Catt thought might be empty spaces.

"I think it is hollow," Catt said. "Like a big cage." she edged closer.

"This spell looks familiar!" Segna exclaimed, "It reminds me of the necromancy I was looking at in the wand... In fact..."

Catt reached out a hand and touched the surface of the sphere. Segna's light was behind her now, so Catt's own shadow was thrown up, enlarged, and distorted on the surface of the thing. Her fingers felt the rough cold texture of iron, confirming her guess.

Segna was mumbling to herself, then she suddenly cried out, "This is it!"

Catt's hand was still resting on a bar of the huge spherical cage, but she turned her head back to look at Segna. "This is what?"

"The other part of the wand's spell! This is the artifact that it connects to when it... *disgorges* the souls!"

"Are you sure?" Catt asked.

"Yes! The words are right here, and these lines must be the continuation of the incomplete ones from the last vellum!" Segna sounded both excited and frightened.

Catt turned back to the sphere and stared at it. Was this where the souls of the dead kings went? Was this where they would have put Segna's soul?

Something inside the cage moved. The quality of the darkness in the lower part of the sphere rippled, the bars vibrated faintly under her fingers.

Catt flinched away, but not before something spoke to her, like a whisper inside her mind, in a voice that was definitely not her own. She had understood it.

"***Help me!***" it had said.

# Caged

Catt felt Segna holding onto her.

"Did you hear it too?" asked Catt.

"Yes!" Segna exclaimed.

Something dark and insubstantial was pressing itself against the inside of the sphere. It seemed to have big eyes. They seemed to blink. It was impossible to tell what it was. It was bigger than a person, but it did not fill the whole space inside the cage.

"What are you?" asked Catt.

The part of it that seemed like eyes became even more eye-like, focusing on her. Nothing like a mouth could be seen, but it spoke again, whispering in a way that Catt could feel inside her head, even though there was no sound.

"***I don't remember!***" It seemed to wail.

"Are you the souls of the dead kings?" Segna asked, voice quavering.

"***No!***" it said, shrinking back, and seeming smaller, "***the souls hurt me! No souls! Help me!***"

"What kind of help do you need?" Catt asked.

"***Help me!***" it repeated.

"Do you want out?" Catt asked.

"***Help me!***" It writhed back and forth.

"Don't let it out!" said Segna.

"I don't know how to let it out!" Catt replied, "and I don't know what it is!"

"***Don't remember!***" it lamented piteously.

"How long have you been trapped here?" Catt asked.

"***So long! So long! So long! So long!***" it seemed to whine.

Segna was still holding on to Catt, but she was looking down now at the spell on the floor at their feet.

"I see words here for *Hurt*, *Contain*, and *Forget*," Segna said. "Look, *Forget* is repeated all around there," she pointed to the base of the sphere.

The thing quieted down, settling restlessly into the bottom of the cage like an animal in a burrow.

"How do we help it?" Catt asked. She was half talking to herself, half to Segna.

"It seems dangerous!" Segna said. "Maybe it is supposed to be trapped here!"

Catt couldn't see where the eyes were anymore, but she still felt like it was watching her.

"We should go!" Segna said, urgently.

Catt let Segna lead her away. When after a few paces, it had not moved or spoken again, Catt turned her back on the sphere. Gripping Segna's hand firmly, she agreed, "Yes! Let's find the way out of here!"

# Egress

The narrow staircase twisted upwards. It seemed to go on forever. Catt and Segna kept holding hands. Segna led with her free hand outstretched, lighting the way. Catt followed, ready to catch Segna if she stumbled. The winding stair was just a little too narrow for them to walk side-by-side.

Suddenly the stair ended. There was thick multi-coloured fabric blocking the way.

They stopped. The muscles in Catt's legs burned from the climb. She could see that Segna was breathing hard.

They rested there for a moment.

When she felt ready, Catt pushed at the cloth. It was heavier and more rigid than a curtain, but it did yield.

Together they pushed, and emerged into a dusty and cluttered room. Catt's heart thrilled at the sudden recognition.

"I know where we are!" she exclaimed.

There were the racks of strange weapons and old armor. There was the ornate but aged glass cabinet where she had found the wand. Its doors were unlocked and half open.

"Where?" asked Segna, looking around in puzzlement. "This doesn't look like any part of the palace that I know."

"It's not the palace," said Catt. "This is the Armory of the Executioner's Guild!"

Segna shuddered.

"No, this is good!" said Catt, "we can escape from here! They'll still be searching for us in the palace."

Segna shook her head in wonder. "I have no idea how the teleportation spell could have carried us this far. It wasn't designed for this kind of distance."

Catt searched around. She found what she was looking for nearby. It was a box full of black robes and hoods. She dragged a couple of them out, but when she saw that the ones underneath were less dusty, she dumped half the box out on the floor. The ones at the bottom of the box were neatly spotless.

"Put this on," Catt said, giving one to Segna and donning another herself. "Running around naked would be pretty conspicuous, but with these, I'll bet nobody will pay much notice to us."

A little further down the rows of shelves, Catt detached some straps from some armor. "These will work as belts," she said, and helped Segna fasten hers.

Next Catt found a sword, and fastened it to the belt, "In case we run into trouble," she said. "do you want one?"

Segna shook her head. "I don't know how to use a sword."

"I think I remember seeing some crossbows closer to the door," Catt suggested.

At a shelf covered with wooden masks, Catt picked up two.

"I don't want to wear that!" Segna said, looking between the masks in Catt's hands and a nearby rack of axes.

"Just for until we get out of the Guild Hall," Catt insisted. "We can ditch them later when we find better disguises."

Segna grudgingly took one mask, but didn't put it on yet, she just gripped it as if trying not to look at it.

Noting Segna's discomfort, Catt held off on putting her own mask on. Best to give her a few minutes to get used to the idea.

Catt led the way towards the door.

"The crossbows were over th–"

Catt stopped short. There was someone sitting in the chair by the fletching table.

The person was dressed in black, with an executioner's mask, but they looked different from the other executioners. Their boots had fine silver trim. There was black-on-black embroidery on their uniform, and their wooden mask was stained dark and was carved to resemble a stylized skull. All of the executioners' masks hinted at the shape of a skull, but this one was blatantly and morbidly skull-like.

The person was motionless. They seemed to be looking directly at Catt.

"Curious," said a cold and inflectionless voice. "How did the two of you get in here?"

"We are... leaving..." Catt said. She nodded towards the door.

The skull-masked person stood slowly and deliberately. They were a head taller than Catt. "I am certain that you are not," they said.

In the corner of her eye, Catt could see Segna inching closer to the door.

The skull turned slightly, "Your Majesty, I recognize you."

"You've been waiting here for us?" Catt asked.

"I am surprised to see you," they said. "I am rarely surprised. How did you get into this place?" they asked again.

Catt countered with a question instead, "What is that thing you have locked up in the cage down below?"

The skull mask shifted back to face Catt again, and it spoke. The voice was deadly calm, "If you tell me how you managed to violate that secret space, I will grant you a quick and painless death."

Catt drew the sword from her belt. She could see that there was no weapon in the skull-masked executioner's hand– yet. An axe was resting against the edge of the table.

"You intend to fight me?" the cold voice began, "It will not–"

Catt didn't wait for them to finish. With a balestra leap and a lunge, she thrust the point of the sword directly into the executioner's chest, and then withdrew it, skipping backwards out of range.

"–do you any good," the cold voice finished, barely glancing down.

Segna gasped. Catt could hear the doorknob rattle as Segna tried it. It was locked.

Catt lunged again, this time stabbing into the black cloth covering the executioner's neck.

"You cannot kill me. You cannot kill what is already dead." The skull-masked executioner picked up their axe. Catt could see bleached white neck bones and a collar bone through the gash her sword had torn in the black cloth.

"Segna get that door open!" Catt urged. The sword she had selected was long, light, and sharp. It was the sort of sword she could fight with most skillfully, but she wasn't sure she could swing it hard enough to break bone.

Segna began to recite a spell. Catt hoped it was something that could shatter the lock.

The skull-masked executioner moved their axe very deliberately, raising it up and resting it against their shoulder like a lumberjack regarding a tree and deciding how to fell it. There was no hint of defensive posturing, as if they did not consider Catt to be a real threat.

The lock clicked, and the door opened. Catt stole a glance at Segna, but she still had her hands up, spell interrupted mid-gesture. The door had been opened from the outside.

In stepped another executioner. He had a short greying beard. In one hand he had a clipboard and in the other was the golden wand.

"Sir, the King escaped–" Crocken began, but he sputtered when he saw Catt. He fumbled for the axe on his belt, dropping both the wand and the clipboard clattering to the floor as he drew the axe. He held it with both hands, defensively, body tense, as if he was acutely aware of the dangers inherent to combat between a light sword and a heavy axe.

"Take the wand and go!" hissed the skull-masked executioner sharply. "I will deal with these two myself!"

"But Sir!" Crocken protested, glancing from Catt to Segna, and back to Catt again, "Let me help you!"

Catt cursed, not only did she have to fight an unkillable undead skeleton, she had to do it while flanked.

Segna had seemed stunned by the arrival of this additional threat, but suddenly she moved, pouncing like a thunderbolt on the fallen wand.

"*Activate!*" shouted Segna.

"**Reveal ench–**" the wand began to say.

"No!" screeched the icy voice of the skull-face, lurching towards Segna, axe upraised.

"*Confirm!*" Segna yelled.

The wand glowed white. Light radiated from the skull-masked executioner as they toppled and collapsed at her feet.

Catt whirled her weapon around to threaten Crocken, who seemed momentarily paralyzed with confusion.

Segna leaped over the heap of black cloth and loose bones and took refuge behind Catt.

"What have you done to our Reaper!?" Crocken wailed.

Catt just kept her sword ready. She wasn't completely certain herself what they had done to the Reaper.

"This wand," Segna said triumphantly, "sucks away the soul of a dead leader!"

Crocken lowered his guard, crouching and prodding at the remains with one hand. Whatever necromancy had animated the Reaper and made it seem like a real person was gone, and it was as if every joint between every bone had disintegrated all at once.

Catt saw the opportunity to dart in and deal a killing blow while Crocken was distracted, but something about his apparent shock and confusion stayed her hand.

"Your Reaper?" Catt asked.

"Our most Senior Executioner," Crocken said. "The leader of our guild."

"Did you know they were an Undead?" Segna asked sharply.

"Exactly *how* Senior was he?" Catt asked.

Crocken seemed not to have registered their questions. He had picked up the dark-wooden skull mask from where it had fallen from the real skull beneath it.

# Memory

Catt followed Segna down the last few steps on the spiral stair and back into the strange subterranean hall where they had seen the spherical cage and its mysterious occupant.

Catt wasn't sure what Segna had in mind— it seemed that they were fleeing in the wrong direction, but Segna seemed filled with purpose, and Catt trusted her. Segna was carrying the wand gripped in her outstretched hand as if she was simultaneously afraid to let go of it, and unwilling to be too close to it.

"I think he's following us," Catt said. She could hear footsteps echoing down the spiral stairwell.

Segna glanced back, looking concerned.

"I can take him if I need to," Catt said.

They ran down the long irregular passageway until they had returned to the huge round cage.

Segna dropped to her knees, and began tracing the engravings on the floor with her finger.

Catt glanced over her shoulder. In the distance, there was a distant spot of green light. Crocken must have emerged from the stairwell with some kind of a lantern.

When her eyes returned to the cage, she saw that the thing inside was stirring. It slowly surged up from where it had been pooled at the bottom, and it seemed to shake itself before it twisted about and pressed against the inside of the cage with its suggestion of a face. It seemed to be regarding them curiously.

"**Nooo! Please, Nooooo!**" It suddenly wailed, thrashing about.

"What?" Catt said in surprise.

Segna glanced up at it. "I'm not going to hurt you," she said.

The thing seemed unconvinced, and continued whipping back and forth in a panic, moaning piteously.

"It's afraid of the wand," said Segna.

Catt nodded, and glanced backwards again. Crocken was much closer now, approaching with his axe in one hand and a magic lantern in the other. His attention seemed to be more focused up at the thing in the cage than at her.

Catt readied her sword, and prepared to fight.

Crocken slowed as he got closer to Catt. He stopped outside of her range. He looked at her, and at the cage, and back to her.

"Don't come any closer," Catt warned.

"***Nooooo!***" whimpered the thing.

"Hush now," said Segna, in a tone that seemed intended to sooth, but that also betrayed her distraction. Catt guessed whatever she was doing required concentration.

"What is that?" Crocken asked.

Catt scoffed, "We're under *your* Guild Hall, what do you think it is?"

"I had no idea this place existed!" he insisted. He started to take a step forward.

"Nope!" Catt flicked the blade up sharply, pointing at his face. "I said no closer!"

Crocken hesitated. "How about if we both put down our weapons," he suggested.

"Counterproposal;" Catt said firmly, "you put down your weapon, I keep mine, and I agree not to kill you just yet."

Crocken stood frozen for a while.

Catt could feel the cool stone under her feet. She could hear Segna mumbling to herself, and the thing in the cage softly sobbing in a soundless voice that went directly into her mind.

Finally, Crocken seemed to come to a conclusion. He backed off a pace, and slowly placed his axe on the floor. Then he carefully skirted around Catt, giving her sword a wide berth, and approached the side of the sphere.

Catt shifted her position to keep herself between him and Segna. Even without his axe, she had to assume he could be dangerous, but for the moment he seemed overwhelmed with curiosity.

Crocken got close to the cage, and as the thing shrank back away from him, he ran the fingers of one hand tentatively along the surface of the cage. Catt began to feel that maybe he had been telling the truth when he claimed to not know about this place.

"Okay," Segna began, "I think I know what to do, but I need... something to write with."

"I don't have anything but this robe and this sword," said Catt.

"What about above? We can go back and look for–"

"Here," said Crocken.

Catt looked. The executioner reached inside a pocket and produced a piece of chalk.

"Wait," Catt said, but Segna had already stood up and was walking over to him.

Catt tensed, gripped with terror that this was a trick, but then Segna had taken the chalk, and she was returning to the engravings on the floor.

Catt watched as Segna decisively scribbled over the word for "Forget" and then on the smooth tile beside it, wrote the Arashan word for "Remember" in neat squared-off Shoming runes.

She did the same for several other parts of the spell. "Wound" was marked over and replaced with "Heal", "Weaken" was replaced with "Restore".

The thing in the cage had grown still while she did this, suggestions of eyes watching her.

Catt was now pretty sure she understood what Segna was doing. She hoped this worked. She hoped this was a good idea.

Segna pointed the wand at the place where the engraved lines of focus converged.

The thing flinched.

"*Disgorge*," commanded Segna.

The wand shuddered in her hand as light blazed out of it, and was sucked into the spell on the floor. The lines lit up with multi-colored ribbons of magic, surging towards the cage.

The thing inside flopped about for an instant, and then seemed to grow a little more substantial. For just a moment its vague dark shape resolved into something less amorphous and more animal-like. In spite of the obscuring mesh of the cage, its body took on a texture like the dark underside of a billowing thundercloud.

When this flurry of magic had spent itself, Catt realized that she had moved to Segna's side without being aware of it.

Crocken had taken several steps away, and he now had his back pressed up against a facet of the wall.

"*I remember something!*" said the thing in the cage. It seemed to sit up straight, head almost centered in the sphere.

Catt realized that the air felt different. More humid.

The eyes of the thing had more definition than they had before. It was clear now that they must really be eyes, even though the position and number of them seemed to drift a little.

"What did you remember?" Catt dared to ask.

A mouth seemed to grin, "***I remembered my name... I am called... Quencher-Of-Campfires!***"

"Why are you here, Quencher-Of-Campfires?" Segna asked.

The grin collapsed, and the eyes rolled, "***I don't remember!***" It moaned.

"How can we help you, Quencher?" Catt asked.

"***I don't know!***" Quencher lamented, sinking lower in the sphere, "***so long! It has been so long!***"

Segna and Catt shared a glance.

Segna said, "I think they have been slowly weakening it with stolen souls, year after year after year."

Catt nodded.

Segna continued, "Perhaps reversing the spell just once can't undo very much."

"Give me back the wand," Crocken said. He was coming closer to them, hand outstretched.

Catt's sword was up in an instant. "No you don't!" she said.

"This *thing* is not part of the guild charter. I must speak with the other Senior Executioners, and find out which of them– if any– knew about what the Reaper was doing down here. I promise you I will get to the bottom of this, but you must give that wand back to me."

Segna shook her head firmly.

"No," Catt verbalized.

Crocken began moving sideways, towards where his axe rested on the floor.

"One more step," Catt threatened, "and your blood spills... all of it."

Crocken hesitated.

"Don't kill him," said Segna. "Let's go. I don't know how to free it, but I don't think he can hurt it anymore without this."

Catt became aware that Quencher-of-Campfires was sitting up again, eyes transfixed upon Crocken's back.

"Okay, let's go," Catt agreed, then to the thing in the sphere, she said, "I'll remember your name, Quencher-Of-Campfires. We'll leave this one here for you."

Crocken looked over his shoulder. He tensed and wobbled slightly as if paralyzed by Quencher's gaze. Perhaps it was just fright.

Catt took the opportunity and tugged on Segna's arm, and they both turned and ran.

# Muddy

Catt and Segna emerged from the main door of the Executioner's Guild Hall. They were both wearing masks, which Segna had consented to when they had gotten up to the armory again.

They had no idea whether Crocken was pursuing them or not.

They had gotten strange looks from a few executioners in the halls, but nobody had stopped them, and now here they were, outside, and seemingly safe for the moment.

The streets were muddy. It looked as if a strong downpour had slurried up all the dry dust of ages. There were puddles all over the streets.

Catt remembered how excited people had become back on that day when a few minutes of drizzle had fallen. This time it was pandemonium. Children were running around the streets splashing in puddles and shouting joyously, but it wasn't just the children. Grown adults were doing it too. Doors and shutters were flung open everywhere. People were leaning out of windows singing songs. someone had abandoned a horse cart in the middle of the street. The horses, manes still drenched, seemed content with this development.

Whatever miraculous clouds had dropped this rain were dissolving away, but shreds of them could still be seen in the sky.

For a moment, Segna seemed to forget all about what they had just gone through. Her face lit up with wonder as they hurried down the street.

A few blocks away and around a few corners, they came across an especially large puddle. It was directly in front of a shop with a large reflective window, and there were half a dozen children of various ages splashing in it.

Segna abruptly tore the wooden mask off of her face, and waded into the puddle. She sank to her knees, and cupped her hands in the water, lifting it up and letting it fall.

Catt stopped too. Her imagination had been running through where to find new disguises, where to find provisions, how to get to them both to the Caravan Depot, and whether she had enough money stashed in her apartment.

Catt waded into the water after Segna, and knelt next to her. She felt the water soaking the fringe of the robe she was wearing.

Segna dipped her hands back into the puddle, swishing them apart, and back together. She seemed to be crying.

Catt took off her own mask. She looked around at the children, they seemed too engrossed in the splashing, and hardly seemed to care that two people dressed like executioners had plopped down in their midsts and taken off their masks.

Catt put her arm around Segna's shoulder.

"Maybe it is a good omen," Segna managed to say. "Maybe we'll get away... maybe they won't catch us..."

Catt squeezed her.

"This place is my home," Segna cried. "I don't want to leave it!"

One of the older children finally seemed to take notice of them, and ushered the smaller ones further down the street to the next big puddle.

Catt wasn't sure what to say, so she just kept clinging to Segna.

Segna's mask floated face down in the puddle like a tiny boat with eye-holes.

"I never thought I would see this, and now I have to leave it." Segna gestured around, beyond the puddle to the evidence of recent rain all around. The sun was gleaming off the wet walls of the buildings.

Catt considered the strange coincidence of the rain.

"Do you know who we met down there?" Catt asked, certainty suddenly blooming in her heart.

Segna looked at Catt.

Catt continued, "That was the Rain God! The nameless one!"

"Quencher-Of-Campfires?" Segna asked.

"Yes!" Catt affirmed, "We know the name of the nameless Rain God!"

Segna looked at her rippling reflection in the puddle, and nodded. "Yes?"

"Maybe we can do something better than running away," Catt suggested. "I know someone who might be able to help us."

# Denomination

The sky was vibrant blue. Yesterday's puddles had been soaked up by the thirsty earth, but there was a hint of it remaining. The city of Great Bakak still *smelled* like rain.

It had been the biggest rain that anyone alive could remember. It logically followed that the Unchurch Against The Nameless Rain God would have to throw the biggest Rain Festival party ever. People were flocking to the Unchurch.

Against this backdrop, the procession led by High Priest Lemmy of the Polypantheonic Temple did not seem quite as unusual as it might have in different circumstances.

Lemmy was wearing his best robes and his tallest hat. Catt followed behind him along with the whole Wailing and Chanting choir in their multi-colored robes and extravagant mismatched hats.

Lemmy and Catt had spent the whole night calling on their eclectic flock of parishioners, while King Segna had hidden in the back room of the Polypantheonic Temple. Now many of these people were part of the procession. Some had come out of respect for High Priest Lemmy's request, and some had come out of simple curiosity.

Catt glanced back. She saw Ms Bethen. She saw Provincial. She saw the green-haired couple with their baby Nikeif whom she had helped christen on her first day as an acolyte. Even Professor Memnestralux was there, walking carefully among the crowd with her wings folded up tight.

The Polypantheonic Temple served so many different worshipers of different gods in different ways, that it was surreal for Catt to see them all together at once.

Beside Catt and Lemmy walked the King. She had no crown and she was wearing an old theatre dress borrowed from Ms Bethen, but Catt thought she looked unmistakably regal.

As they reached the square, and approached the Unchurch, Catt stole a glance at Segna, to see whether or not she was looking at the palace. There it was across the park and up the terraces. Segna was not looking at it. She was looking ahead, an expression of determination on her face.

There were throngs of people all around the Unchurch, but people parted aside and made way for High Priest Lemmy.

Up the steps, and inside the Unchurch. There, seated, were the blue-clad congregation of the Unchurch's members. They seemed restless, and the reason why was readily apparent. The dignitaries and priests of other temples were seated in their places of honor along the sides of the sanctuary, the judges of the high court were there in their places, but the throne reserved for the King was conspicuously empty.

As Lemmy's procession invaded the sanctuary and moved up the right-hand aisle, heads turned to see what the disruption was.

Catt saw that all the advisor's chairs around the empty throne were also empty. Catt recognized the Chief Admonisher standing behind the throne with a frown on their face, which melted into astonishment when they spotted King Segna.

At the pulpit in the front of the Unchurch, the Anti-bishop was in conversation with the Seneschal of Delays and two Senior Executioners. From their builds and bearings, Catt could tell that neither one of them was Crocken.

The Anti-bishop appeared aghast at whatever they were telling him, and all four of them seemed further startled when Lemmy spoke in a voice that seemed too big for his tiny frame.

"Greetings, to all of you, and blessings to you from *every* god!" Lemmy seemed to be addressing the blue-clad un-worshipers just as much as he was speaking to the Anti-bishop.

"What is the meaning of this!" the Anti-bishop sputtered.

"Her Majesty, King Segna Ur-Segna has something to tell you all about the Rain God!" Lemmy declared.

The Anti-bishop seemed speechless at this breach in protocol. The executioners and the Seneschal of Delays stared at Segna.

"Quencher-Of-Campfires!" Segna proclaimed in a bold clear voice. "The name of the Nameless Rain God is Quencher-Of-Campfires!"

There was a collective gasp from the congregation followed by a susurration of whispers.

"How dare you!" cried the Anti-bishop, "this is an affront to our affrontery! A blaspheme against our blasphemy! It shall not stand!"

Catt saw that both executioners had taken several steps down towards Segna. Catt moved to position herself in front of Segna protectively.

"The King has been declared faithless!" shouted one of the executioners. "Don't listen to her!"

Catt's pulse quickened, and her hand went to the sword at her belt.

High Priest Lemmy stepped in front of the executioners, tiny arms raised, "You, loyal executors of the law, need to listen to this as well!"

Catt was surprised to see them falter and stop.

Segna continued, "Consider that the Rain God doesn't hate you, the Rain God was simply unable to bring rain." She was addressing the congregation, ignoring the Anti-bishop. "Perhaps the Rain God would have heard our prayers, and the prayers of our ancestors, had the god not been weakened intentionally by malicious magic!"

"Lies!" screeched the Anti-bishop, "filthy dessicated lies!"

Segna ignored him. She lifted the wand up over her head. Catt watched the two executioners. Their masked faces followed it.

"The evidence is here in this wand!" Segna asserted. "Here in this wand, and in the hidden catacombs underneath the Executioners Guild Hall!" Segna then turned towards the place where the Judges of the High Court were sitting, "I demand an investigation into the enslavement and oppression of our Rain God, Quencher-Of-Campfires!"

"A faithless King is in no position to demand anything!" shouted one of the executioners.

"Yes, why should we heed this wild accusation?" asked one of the Judges.

Segna looked frustrated, but defiant, "Give this wand to necromancy experts from the University! The proof is inside."

"That wand is the property of the guild!" declared the executioner.

Catt began to sing; "*Quencher-Of-Campfires,*

*Please give to us a sign!*

*Show us you can hear us!*

*Please do not forsake us,*

*And we will not forsake you...*"

Catt felt like her voice was so tiny in the huge space. She felt like she was singing off-key, and she knew the words had no rhythm to them. When she first opened her mouth, she had felt afraid that everyone would stare at her, but as she continued, she realized it would be so much worse if everyone ignored her.

Segna wasn't ignoring her. Their eyes met. Segna seemed surprised that Catt was singing, but almost immediately, she started singing too, trying to follow along, which made the song sound even more awkward, because Catt was just making up the words as she went along.

Lemmy, and the whole Wailing and Chanting choir joined in, and a small cacophony began, as the rest of the whole Unchurch fell deeply silent.

*"This will be the last thing I do,"* though Catt as she repeated Quencher-Of-Campfires' name discordantly. *"In a minute they'll be cutting us to pieces."* But instead of drawing her sword, she reached for Segna's hand, and kept on singing.

Another sound started. It was coming from outside. The crowds outside the Unchurch were suddenly cheering and shouting and laughing.

"Rain!" someone shouted from the door.

Segna whirled to the Anti-bishop. "Open the skylight!" she commanded, "There's your god now! Open the skylight!"

"Never!" raged the Anti-bishop. "You will cease this desecration!"

But the silence that had bound the blue-clad congregation was broken. There was a roar of voices. Many people jumped up from their seats. Some pushed towards the door, trying to see the rain. Some began shouting along with the Wailers and Chanters. Some shouted, "Open the skylight!"

Catt heard a few screams, and looked over her shoulder. She saw Provincial opening up his backpack, and hundreds of tightly coiled bundles of wires were unfurling themselves and stretching upward and outward like an expanding cloud of smoke.

People cringed out of Jangley's way, but Jangley was not there to hurt anyone, Jangley was gripping the ornate columns and carved walls and climbing upwards. Catt could see the small canister of the golem's head as it rose, bobbing, all the way up to the high-arched ceiling, where with the strength of dozens of animated wires, they forcefully pried the skylight open.

Rain began to fall directly into the Unchurch Against The Nameless Rain God, nameless no longer. There was pandemonium. Blue-clad un-worshipers danced in the column of downpour, transforming themselves into worshipers. The Anti-bishop sank to his knees, shouting, face livid, eyes bulging, ignored and unheard by anyone.

Catt wrapped her arms around Segna, "They heard us!"

The rain was intensifying. So was the noise.

Segna pressed her face into Catt's neck. Segna's shoulders were heaving, whether from crying or laughter, Catt couldn't even tell. She just hung on.

As Catt stood locked in an embrace with her love, she watched Lemmy clapping his hands, perhaps trying to bring rhythm to the riot. She saw old Ms Smink wailing joyously at the sky. She saw the High Judges, pushing and jostling like children to get closer to the falling curtain of rain water. She saw one of the executioners, standing on the edge of the column of rain from the skylight, daring to take off their mask just long enough to let a few drops fall on their bare face.

Catt turned her eyes back to Segna, and for a while saw only her.

## Year's End

The year was coming to an end, and the people of Great Bakak were gathered in the square in front of the royal palace for the Regicide Festival.

Some things had changed, and some things were the same.

An orchestra was playing. The long tables were set up on the terraces. People wore brightly colored clothes, and hats ranging from the dazzling to the absurd, but this year there were a lot of colorful umbrellas in the crowd, after all, it might rain!

People were feasting and enjoying the generosity of the King, but on the average, the food was a little less extravagant than usual. All the great kitchens had been disrupted by the expansion of the Unburning, and the establishment of a new Smokefields further away from the city was an on-going process that affected the availability of all hot food.

The noise of festivity was suddenly interrupted by a sudden low thrumming note. One of the three musicians on the palace steps was relentlessly and fluidly drawing an enormous bow across a large stringed instrument. The time had come.

King Segna Ur-Segna was still seated. She had not touched her glass of wine. It did not contain the usual poison and potion of sedation, it was just ordinary wine, but she had not wanted to drink it.

The two Senior Executioners walked solemnly, and somewhat awkwardly around the table where the King and her Consort sat.

A Judge of the High Court stood up from the neighboring table and joined them.

"The King is Dead!" said one executioner in voice that was booming, but not confident.

"–Symbolically!" amended the Judge. "The Execution of King Segna Ur-Segna is hereby delayed," the Judge consulted a small slip of paper, "for three hundred and ninety six years, one for each minute of rain that fell during her tenure as King!"

There was a scattering of applause. There were whispers. Some people grumbled at this overturning of age-old traditions.

A pair of porters approached carrying an enormous orange gourd.

King Segna stood. She removed her crown and placed it on the table in front of her.

The porters placed the gourd on the table also.

Segna, no longer a King, took the hand of Catt, no longer a Consort, and they walked away from the table, not looking back.

At that moment, the other two musicians on the palace steps began furiously carving a melody from their instruments. The first deep note was still there, and now added to it was a frenetic sorrowfully refrain that seemed to be entirely composed of tones and timbres calculated to tug at one's emotional core.

One of the executioners raised their axe high, and brought it down, and with a gout of juice and pulp and a splatter of seeds, the gourd was split cleanly in two.

Some people in the crowd muttered. Some cheered. A few laughed.

The other executioner quickly unfurled a black cloth and covered the pieces of gourd. They hastily placed the crown on top of the cloth, as if they were eager to get this part of the ceremony over and done with.

Then the four coronation dancers approached. The music changed, the dance of the Royal Lots began, and the crowd seemed to become unanimous again. This was the way the Regicide Festival was supposed to feel. The old king was gone with the old year, the new King would usher in the New Year. The new King might be anyone.

# Epilogue

A fruit tree is growing in the alleyway next to a five story apartment in the Poor Quarter. Its roots push aside flagstones and twist around the rusty water pump, unneeded and forgotten.

The tree had grown from a sprouted seed pit that fell from the window of the top floor. A Priest Of Many Gods and a Retired King live there. It is a humble place for such important women, but the tree is not concerned with them.

It just drinks the sunlight, and drinks the rain water that soaks into the stony soil. Ants scurry up and down its trunk. Sometimes it feels the weight of the children who climb up it to fetch down the spicy red fruit that grows in its branches. They carry away the seeds, and sometimes plant them. Some day there will be a forest here in this city.

*The End*